# Orion You Came and You Took All My Marbles

# Orion You Came and You Took All My Marbles

Kira Henehan

milkweed
editions

© 2010, Text by Kira Henehan
All rights reserved. Except for brief quotations in critical articles or reviews, no part of this book may be reproduced in any manner without prior written permission from the publisher: Milkweed Editions, 1011 Washington Avenue South, Suite 300, Minneapolis, Minnesota 55415 (800) 520-6455
www.milkweed.org

Published 2010 by Milkweed Editions
Printed in Canada
Cover design by Christian Fuenfhausen
Interior design by Rachel Holscher
The text of this book is set in Sabon.
10 11 12 13 14   5 4 3 2 1
First Edition

Please turn to the back of this book for a list of the sustaining funders of Milkweed Editions.

Library of Congress Cataloging-in-Publication Data
Henehan, Kira, 1974–
    Orion you came and you took all my marbles / Kira Henehan. — 1st ed.
        p.    cm.
    ISBN 978-1-57131-075-0 (pbk. : alk. paper)
    I. Title.
    PS3608.E545O75 2010
    813'.6—dc22
                                                    2009046701
This book is printed on acid-free paper.

for Ryan

# Orion You Came and You Took All My Marbles

# Preamble

**It was Binelli's brainchild** and only he knew all the specifics. Many many lists were involved. They were drawn up, copied, distributed, et cetera, with the terse minimum of words regarding the next set of Assignments and travel arrangements. We waited for them like someone might wait for something else. Christmas say, or aurora borealis. Dawn. The lists told us the what and where and when of it all, which in this particular instance were specifically and respectively: pillows, in the center lane of fifty-two lanes, and night.

The first had some leeway.

For instance, when I realized that hauling away all the unusually heavy pillows meant there'd be no pillows on the bed for when we returned, for certainly we would return, eventually, at Binelli's of course discretion, I sent Murphy back with the blue one. He dug up from god knows where some old baseball jerseys in exchange, and that seemed to go over okay. Although I found that I also kind of liked the jerseys, all shrunken yellow arms and age-cracked words and the like. I held one up against myself even, to suggest perhaps that a jersey, just one, should be mine, but no one took notice or commented favorably on yellow being my color and the size, though made for young boys, being perfectly suited to my frame. And I couldn't be greedy and Binelli had his eye on me anyhow.

—Binelli, I said to him, nodding casually.

—Finley, he said back with an equivalent head gesture.

We suspect him of being connected.

I've come to think he may in fact be dreamy as well and would sometimes not much mind maybe cranking it up a notch or two between us, but there was right then the plan to consider and right then I imagined he needed all his faculties intact.

Though there's nothing, I imagine, still to this day, quite so effective as a girl in a little boy's baseball jersey to set hearts to racing. Or some other anatomical specific.

Though racing would not then seem quite right.

Call to attention, perhaps.

Neither here nor there. I had no jersey, we were short one pillow, and I've found over the course of my admittedly limited experience that an overall sense of just-having-lifted-oneself-from-a-dip-in-the-lake dampness provides much the same stimulation any one article of clothing could. I keep a spray bottle and some thin white T-shirts close at hand.

# Addendum
# to Preamble

**I kept also,** I might as well admit at this point for the sake of accuracy, the jersey, on the sly.

I am terribly covetous.

# 1

**It was all over gravel,** but better than the last place. There was all over swampland and crocodiles.

# 2

**At the designated location** were many men of pleasing *visage*.

But if one begins with such a high class of word, a word in need of italic, of accent, one can hardly go on with the report. The stakes upped, as it were.

There were many men of pleasing countenance.

Aspect?

Many, anyway. So many so as to be unusual; on occasion there might be one; two, rarely; but here so many as to be unusual. I had to wonder. I was confused, besotted in no less than nine different directions. Confusion made me suspect, suspicion made me paranoid, paranoia made me appear insane, insanity made me desirable, and from no less than nine different directions did the eyes fall upon me. Centered as I was at a central table, and so desirable with insanity.

I am not desirable.

It's no single thing.

I have red hair and no freckles. The hair is straight as the edge of a page. There are other things, but I offer these three to illustrate the nature of the difficulty: I lack the appropriate combinations. Red hair is acceptable if freckles are involved. If there are no freckles but only a broad expanse of milky skin, one should be curly. Et cetera. I excused myself with perhaps an excess of formality. I used excuses that clashed and contradicted one another. I, I dare say, protested too much. I took my leave.

Binelli found me. He finds us all, every time. I should likely not have stopped so soon for a shrimp cocktail, but the stand was right there, all the little shrimps so pink and pearly.

—Finley, he said.

—Binelli, I said back.

We maintained a brief but meaningful standoff. I can win any such standoff. I can win any contest involving silence or stillness or maintaining a straight face. I once, presumably out of some heartfelt anger, maintained a silence for so long I forgot who I was. With speech went character, with character memory, with memory me. All I can recall from that time was the feeling of being something very very small, encased within some sort of roomy cocoon. I was erased entirely; that was before Binelli gave me the new papers. We stood off and Binelli lost.

—Finley, he said. —I need you to go back in there and talk to this guy.

—Which guy, I wondered. There were so many, all of such pleasing aspect.

—He's in the back right corner. He runs Up All Puppets!

—What.

—Up All Puppets!

—Did. You. Say. I continued as if he hadn't interrupted and then there was again silence, it being unclear whose turn it was to speak. The question having already been answered, as it were.

Again, a standoff. Again, my victory.

—Up All Puppets!

I tried to remain calm. —I will not.

—But you will.

—Puppets, I informed Binelli, —are my Most Hated Thing.

—Not so. He considered for a moment. —Not so at all. What about the Russians?

He had me there. I had no love for the Russians. Less than no love. A negative value of love. Despite my Russian papers and my tidy grasp of the Russian tongue.

—That being as it may, I told him, —Puppets are right up there.

—No, he said. —No, I think you hate that girl dressed in blue a little bit more than Puppets.

He was slick. I did, I did with every fiber of my being hate that girl dressed in blue more than Puppets, although no more certainly than the Russians. I hated also to concede but concede I did.

She was simply too tall, too gregarious. Too easy with her affections.

—Well then, he continued, —Puppets are—and only if there's nothing I'm forgetting—third on your list of Most Hated Things. Let me, if I may, offer a parallel.

I let him.

—You, he told me, —are one of *my* Most Hated Things. I find you utterly and irrevocably despicable.

I nodded. This was no secret.

—However, he said, —you know as well that Murphy is, to my thinking, a notch or two ahead of you in despicability. Irredeemable despicability. And then, you are also aware, I find The Lamb perhaps more despicable than that. Making you, you *Finley,* third on my list of Most Hated Things. Which is why you, and neither Murphy nor The Lamb, are being Assigned the Third-Worst Assignment.

—Up All Puppets!? I said, quite unnecessarily.

—Indeed. Now, should you refuse, as I'm sure you will not, you will rise in despicability and therefore be Assigned perhaps the Second- or even First-Worst Assignment. Having risen in the ranks, so to speak. Would you like to know what the Second- and First-Worst Assignments entail?

His smile was such that I didn't.

# 3

**I went back into the bar** and cast my eyes about the men. I tried not to swoon. There was a man in the back right corner, alone at a table. Alone, that is, but for a decanter of what one might reasonably assume to be beer, if one were the assuming type.

—What are you drinking, I said, sliding in beside him.

He looked me up and down. I took the opportunity to glance casually about the area for Puppets. I saw none but that didn't mean there weren't any. Who knows how these Puppet men operate. I maintained an aura of alertness. He was of such pleasing aspect.

—Look, I'm not really—

I put a finger to my lips. —No need to explain. I'm only here to work out some details.

I sniffed at the decanter. It was indeed beer. I signaled the barman for an extra glass. Beer tends to smooth out those initial awkwardnesses.

—First, I told him, as I waited for my glass to arrive, —I have to ask that you not suddenly pull out your Puppets. I was Assigned to this job, and I am prepared to carry it out with all appropriate aplomb and enthusiasm, but I have to admit to a certain distaste,

I said in a polite way of putting it mildly, —for the fundamental tools of your profession.

He'd been hitting the pitcher hard, evidently, awaiting my arrival; the confusion on his face could not be masked. Or perhaps it wasn't confusion. Perhaps there was a confidence scheme at work and he didn't want it widely known that he was the man behind Up All Puppets! Perhaps there were enemies or competitors close at hand. An elderly Indian gentleman a bit farther back in the corner was looking upon us with what seemed an excess of interest. I glared for a moment and then turned back to the Puppet Man.

I nodded sagely at his blank stare.

—I understand, I assured him. —You maybe have a code name you'd prefer? Something we could use to make the conversation subtle yet smooth, insofar as we'd know to what each of us was referring, while keeping our neighbors (a dark glare again at the not yet chastened neighbor) in the dark?

He shrugged his acquiescence, but offered no alternative.

I thought long and hard. —How about 'firewood?' I said.

The Puppet Man was a cagey one; he neither argued nor assented. It occurred to me that Binelli might have offered up a bit more information before throwing me into the Assignment, but Binelli would only have said that it was my job to gather the pertinent information. My job to suck, as it were, the details from the tight-lipped party. Like snake-poison from a big toe. I used the necessary imaginative tools at my disposal. I leaned in.

The glass I'd requested was smacked down on the table by the thin-hipped barman at that very moment, averting any possibility of sucking for the time being. Informational or otherwise. I poured a generous helping of the beer and offered to refill the Puppet Man's glass.

—Look, he said, holding a hand up.

I stopped pouring. I looked up. He shook his head impatiently and motioned for the pouring to continue.

I wondered if the Puppet Man was in some way impaired.

He took a long drink from his glass of beer and set it back on the table. —Look, he said again. —I just got out of something and I don't really—

—Whoa! I told him, holding up my own hands. —I have to ask that you maintain some sort of professionalism here. You are, I admit, a man of very pleasing countenance, and under different circumstances I might allow temptation to overtake my duties. And I can certainly, I said, —understand your own attraction, but let me please assure you that it is based solely on illusion; I am not at all desirable. I am only confused and therefore appear slightly insane, which I understand is quite attractive to the average male. Not to imply that you are at all average, per se, but only that I understand your willingness to throw caution to the wind and attempt to entice me into drunken foreplay. My first priority however, I said, —is the Assignment, as I'm sure beneath your animal impulses your priority rests as well. Therefore, I will ask that we hold off the flirting, kissing, fondling, et cetera, until we've come to some sort of agreement regarding the Puppets.

He looked slightly mortified.

—I've embarrassed you, I said apologetically, without really apologizing. I'd meant every word and knew that as soon as he was out from under my sway he too would realize the wisdom of my lecture. —Please understand, this is not a direct rebuke of your affections, only a holding off until such a time as they would be more appropriate. Perhaps after another decanter or two of beer, when the business is completed to our mutual satisfaction. Agreed?

I held up my glass to cheer his, but Binelli roared up to the table before the chastened Puppet Man could even toast.

—Finley.

—Binelli.

—What the hell do you think you're doing, he wondered.

—My Assignment. Or did you forget you put me on Puppets?

—This, he pointed a shaking finger at my recalcitrant drinking companion, —is not Mr. Uppal.

—Mr. Who.

—Mr. Uppal. Of Uppal Puppets. The elderly Indian gentleman

who has been waiting with all patience for your arrival at his table. The hors d'oeuvres he's ordered have gotten cold. The fine artisinal champagne has become warm. His spirits are low and his ire is raised. So what, I again wonder, the hell do you think you're doing flirting with this lacrosse-team remnant here.

The target of this last comment bristled a bit at the implied slight but we paid him no mind. I took a second look at the Indian gentleman who had earlier been on the receiving end of my finest, frostiest glare. He gave me a slight nod and raised a dangerously overfilled champagne flute in our direction.

A little bit became clear.

Then, as I considered further, a little bit more.

—I see, I told Binelli. —Mr. Uppal. Of Uppal Puppets. Indian gentleman. Yes.

—Would you please now wait for me outside. I recognized the quality of barely controlled rage in his voice, particularly when bumped up against the polite tone he used to next address the Puppet Man-turned-Lacrosse-Team Remnant. —Please excuse this *Finley*. She knows not what she does.

Now barely controlled rage welled up in me. I knew what I did. I knew and did it well. I used all the tricks, the full arsenal of wiles bestowed upon members of my species and sex. I had been, simply, misinformed. I drank half my mug of beer in one long swallow before flouncing out into the daylight.

# 4

**Murphy found me** collecting myself in the doorway. He smelled of sun and of something else, synthetics perhaps. Perhaps something else. Those were great gray days.

It was probably not his fault.

Things stick to Murphy, things and other things like people. For instance: If three of us—say me, Binelli, and Murphy—were to be coated in honey and tied to a post, and a hive of bees were to be slashed open, the bees would settle on Murphy. He would be covered in honey, and covered in bees, and covered in welts. He would be filled with fear and pain. It was probably not his fault, whatever that other smell was. I could overlook it. I took the bad with the good.

—Was that lacrosse-team remnant you were sitting with the Up All Puppets! guy, he said.

—Evidently not, I said.

—Then who was it?

—Someone who was not the Up All Puppets! guy.

The smell was rankling me a bit. It wasn't, I was sure, Murphy's fault, but nonetheless I became ever so slightly brusque. Where had he found sun. Those were great gray days, smelling of any number of things. Sun not being one.

He shrugged. —I didn't think so, he said, unwarrantedly smug.

Binelli interrupted before I had the chance to shun Murphy viciously.

—Finley, he said.

—Murphy, he added.

—Binelli, we said in a remarkable unison that must have pleased Binelli to no end. Love of order, all that. His face softened ever so slightly.

—Finley, Mr. Uppal has agreed to a brief meeting over a not-even-close-to-inexpensive bottle of port I've ordered for his table. The cost of which will, incidentally, be withheld from your wages.

Wages?

—So if you would please get back in there with all due haste, he suggested, —we can begin to repair the damage your ineptitude has so far caused this Investigation.

I paused, wondering if this was not perhaps the best time to wonder aloud about these wages he'd mentioned.

Binelli clapped his hands sharply in front of my face however, not just once but three times, in rapid succession. —Now? he said in a way that sounded like but was certainly not a question. I nodded quickly and made for the door.

# 5

**You see then why a report** becomes necessary.

You see how the tiniest misunderstanding is conflated. How with more information. How the meeting had been conducted, nonetheless, information or no, almost none whatsoever, with the utmost precision and professionalism. How precisely and professionally, subsequently, I have narrated the events. *Transcribed*. How henceforth it will be simply a matter of pulling a precise and professional and perhaps quite creatively fastened sheaf of pages from my satchel, and locating the moment in question, and pointing a stern and righteously trembling finger at that precisely and professionally transcribed moment, and being redeemed. Rewarded. Regaled with praise for keeping such a fine account.

However tedious to keep it may already be proving.

# 6

Whereupon such tedium, offered an inch, begs mightily, merci-
lessly, for a yard, and I am compelled to gesture—with a great
and profound reluctance, somewhat wishing reports had never
been started—toward that great tedious time between my waking and today, rendering, one can only hope, further digression
unnecessary.

So:

Murphy came after I was already there. He came of his own
accord.

I too may well have come of my own accord; I may always have
been there, but Murphy definitely was not always there, and as far
as I can ascertain was not summoned/dragged/blackmailed/et cetera. I remember the day he came. It had not been sunny then either and, as would make sense, he did not carry any smell of sun
about his person.

Whence the sun smell.

I wonder.

I also digress. From the digression itself as it were. He came
and he was absorbed without formality into us. Maybe he had
been expected. Binelli introduced him to me as Murphy. He didn't
look like a Murphy, like what I at least would expect a Murphy

to look like. And apparently I didn't look much like a Finley to him, because when Binelli introduced us (Murphy, Finley; Finley, Murphy), Murphy said, —Finley?

And Binelli said, —Sure, why not?

So.

When Binelli had retreated behind his door, Murphy stared and stared at me. I was made slightly anxious by this, until I realized the probable cause. —My eyes, I acknowledged.

He nodded quickly.

—Are yellow, I finished.

—Yes, he said.

—I don't know why, I said. —They just are.

—Yes, he said.

Then he said, —It's very unusual, yellow eyes.

Then he said, —Why do they call you Finley.

—Why do they call you Murphy, I answered, not really answering, having ultimately no surefire explanation.

—I suppose, he said, —it's my name?

He said it like a question and looked at me closely. For what, who knew. Perhaps an answer. Perhaps not. The eyes I am aware can be distracting. Binelli had said so at least. The Lamb had as well, had in fact on several occasions pronounced them nightmare-making.

—Try not to look at them, I offered. —If they bother you.

—They don't bother me, he said. —*Finley,* he said. He shuffled something in his pockets which was, I would soon come to learn, a regular thing he did. Stick his hands in his pockets and jangle around in there. And rock a bit back and forth, and look down at the ground, and hum a little three-note tune. All these things he did on a regular basis. A nervous set of habits I supposed.

—Okay then, *Finley,* he said, pronouncing my name with what I may or may not be paranoid in assuming to be a touch of distaste.

It's not a terrible name. It's not something, at least, I can help. I was *named,* as people generally are, and the naming forces were beyond my control.

Did I mention yet that Binelli made me a Russian? By way of my papers, he did. He did that knowing full well my feelings on the matter. This is important to say now because Murphy asked where it was from, *Finley*.

I said I didn't know, but my papers made me Russian. And then he laughed and laughed and laughed. —Russian? he said over and over. —Russian?

And then he stopped laughing all of a sudden and said, —That figures, and then that was all for our first conversation. We've had many since then. And with the tyrannically needy tedium thus appeased, there I'll let the digression end.

# 7

**Mr. Uppal, Professor** Uppal—the correction had been made over introductions and then flogged to death throughout the port course each and every single time I referred to him thereafter as Mister, with admittedly a sort of autistic inability to make the mental change required to correct the salutation—born Early Uppal, was late.

# 8

**On the matter** of Mr. Uppal:

*Professor* Uppal:

Born Early Uppal, year unknown, but one could surmise a good fifty-to-sixty-to-sixty-five years ago and count painfully backward and guess at a decade, if one were to care enough to go through the trouble.

I perhaps should, but do in fact not.

Care.

Enough or to.

It would only, after all, require yet another unnecessary digression, this time involving maths no less, for which other reports may happily clear room, encourage, even, with their tidy charts and year-end projections and cheerful calculations but for which this report has no time. Starting already behind, as it were, and not inclined in the least to frivolity.

He was to have been more grandly named, this young Uppal, this first Uppal child to result from the union of Singh and Elda Uppal (née Holliday); he was also, however, to have been more grandly born and thus deserving, poor creature, of the imposing and unwieldy moniker which was to have been bestowed upon his squalling brown head. For Singh and Elda Uppal had conceived, right alongside this hopeful fetus, a plan to rise swiftly and with a certain irascible fervor through the ranks of high society—not the shabby high society of their native land either, no, but of a society whose very dregs outshone the royalty of their own high society in immeasurable wattage. And the ease with which this rising was to occur seemed so simple, such a no-brains-necessary sort of plot, that they looked upon their neighbors and friends with a scorn that increased as quickly and magnificently as Elda's girth—more so, even, as she was a slip of a woman to begin, and though nearly doubling in weight through the abbreviated course of her pregnancy, did so with such delicate subtlety that it hardly from day to day seemed as though an expansion was occurring at all.

Pride goeth before a fall is, I have little doubt, an expression that has been translated into their and likely every known language of all the lands, but like most people, it simply never occurred to the Uppals that their disdain for their peers would ever stick out a stocky well-fed limb to trip them. Theirs was a disdain they took no pains whatsoever to hide, as they packed their meager possessions and ate grandly and without regard for the future their rations of rare delicacies and as Elda blew their scrappy savings on the finest silks available at market and sewed herself into the most magnificent saris and other, more unusual, articles of clothing, patterns copied from coveted, covertly passed-about photographs from lands afar, smudged and worn from the many eager fingers of the village's would-be fashionistas and sharp-tongued naysayers alike.

No one perhaps related to them either the fable of a certain grasshopper and ant, and the point would certainly have been lost on them anyway, neither Uppal resembling in the slightest a grasshopper and cautionary tales generally most effective at any rate *before* the idea against which one is being cautioned has been fertilized and is gaining heft and weight with the merciless momentum of an unborn baby.

They had spent almost their last monies on two one-way tickets out. Out of town, out of country, headlong toward a land where a baby's birth granted papers and all the rights and privileges thereof not only to a baby but to parents who'd after all proved their worth by concocting such an intelligent scheme in the first place. The papers—which Singh hoped quietly would be edged in powdered gold—were the baby's right and due, born with no decision or malicious forethought upon the host country's terra firma, and more of a *reward* to the parents, for keen demonstration of industry and ambition, two of the land in question's most respected ideals. The Uppals were ripe with industry and ambition, and ripe with child and ripe with impressive sympathy-girth—Singh had put on more weight than his wife, with the lavish lifestyle they enjoyed in those salad days of incubation and the devil-may-care plunderage of their resources—and felt more and more as though the country they were invading would be *grateful* for their company.

And it was on the very day of what they had come to think of as their triumphant crossing to the land of milk and honey, the land of the gilded paper ticket to the fair, their ticker-tape parade homecoming, that the one factor they had relied on for their free pass, the small seed that had bore such industrious fruit of ingenuity, became their ruin. Elda's water broke, two months early, in the carriage on the way to the station, and, though she tried valiantly to forge ahead, braving the humiliation of a soaking sari and screaming impressively at the ladies and then the men and then the armed and amused guards who stood between her and the last and most imperative step in her path to glory and riches, she was denied admission and birthed instead the impatient baby in a customs office, attended by three disgusted and impeccably turned-out cabin hostesses who spoke throughout of the atrocities being inflicted on their brand-new uniforms and who would likely be held responsible for damages.

I do not know who was held responsible for the atrocitied uniforms.

What is clear however is that the child, with more good-natured humor than one would expect from the foiled and frustrated pair of Uppals, was called simply Early instead of the string of successively impressive names originally chosen, the many initials of which had been already sewn into silken baby clothes with golden thread and which E.U. would wear without confusion for the duration of his babyhood.

*P.U.* I suppose. His preference, not mine.

# 9

**On the occasion** of my second meeting with Mr. Uppal, *Professor*
Uppal, a meeting for which I was one hundred percent more prepared, having been armed, as it were, with at last the proper details
of place and name and time et cetera, without which one might as
well send in an *amateur,* I was received with exemplary formality
by a uniformed manservant and deposited into the hands of Dame
Uppal.

Dame Uppal was what one might refer to as a Handsome Woman, which has never to me seemed much of a compliment. I do
not, therefore, mean to suggest a compliment by my use of the term.
Handsome is not something a woman should be.

I passed the time awaiting Early's late arrival in a sitting room
with Dame Uppal. She did not offer me snacks, sodas, canned
fruits, trays of meats—cured or otherwise—or anything much in
the way of hospitality.

She instead lay on the divan a sort of meticulous disarray.
If you find this suggestive of nothing so much as an oxymoron,
you are reading correctly. Catching my drift, so to speak. She lay
on the divan as if disarrayed on *purpose*—hair fetchingly disheveled; scanty nightclothes not quite covering as much of her legs as
one might prefer, if one were not some manner of fetish-magazine

deviant; lipstick as if recently ravished right across her mouth and so forth. Yet her limbs had none of the languor such disarray would suggest. She did not seem loose on pills or drink. She did not seem quite mad, or even mildly perturbed. She spoke, when she spoke, which was in fact much sooner than this laborious descriptive passage might lead one to believe, with dignity and care.

—You are my husband's colleague, she said. —From the University, or one of Binelli's?

—One of Binelli's, I said. —Not the Most Hated, either.

I don't know why I felt the need to elaborate in that particular way. It wasn't a statement intrinsically bound to elevate one in another's estimation. And why I might even deign to gain this woman's respect or approval, I'm sure I have no idea. She was not important insofar as my objective. She was not a vital contact I was obliged to woo. She was not the bearer of snacks, sodas, canned fruits, trays of meats—cured or otherwise. She was merely the wife, the dizzy broad, zonked out, to all appearances, on the divan, left to entertain Mr. Uppal's 'colleague' as he freshened up.

Yet I said it, and was undeniably pleased to see her thoughtful nod.

# 10

Binelli had been there when I came out of the silence. Or maybe he brought me out. Maybe he was there all along.

Either way.

I opened my eyes, or maybe they had already been open.

Again, either way.

But when things focused properly, Binelli was there.

—Tea? he said.

I said yes, but my voice was rusty. Who knew how long it had been since its services were needed. I mouthed yes and then nodded to make clear that I was being affirmative and agreeable. Even then I could tell that Binelli was not to be trifled with.

The tea helped. There was honey. The tea and/or the honey made things right.

—You'll be needing new papers, Binelli said. —Finley, he added with such extraordinary nonchalance that I didn't even think to question.

We drank the tea. We made bland small talk to get my voice awoken and up to speed. The Lamb drifted through and glared at me, then drifted through again and managed a grimace, then finally sat down and had some tea.

Binelli introduced me to her as Finley. He introduced her to me as The Lamb. There was no basis upon which to argue either point.

We made some small talk, me and The Lamb.

This was all before Murphy. Murphy came later, as previously reported, presumably of his own accord.

—You can sleep out here, Binelli told me, when all the tea was drunk and the small talk taxed. He pointed to the couch on which I was already sitting. He pointed then to a small pile of sheets. They were green sheets, like the Tropics. It was hot in the room but the sheets made things seem cool. —We'll get you your papers tomorrow.

—Am I Russian, I wondered.

—You don't appear to be, Binelli said.

The Lamb made a face as if to suggest my being Russian was the most absurd idea she'd yet come across.

—Good, I said. —I *hate* the Russians. I had no basis for this either, but it was something I knew from somewhere deep inside. Maybe a memory that had been slow or stubborn and hadn't left with the rest. Or maybe not a memory at all but a new kind of fact, of which there might be more, revealing themselves at whim, over time.

There were in fact more. They did reveal themselves at whim. I couldn't know that then, but I was aware of the possibility.

—I see, said Binelli, making surely a mental note of this innate distaste that he would, no later than The Very Next Day, use against me. For no apparent reason that I can yet see other than sheer spite.

But that evening I could not have known that Binelli was filled with spite, as full as most people are filled with blood. Binelli and The Lamb retired behind a door that was shut behind them and locked with a series of brisk clicks. I took the top sheet from the small pile and made to shake it out, but before I had even made one shake I looked again at what I thought I had seen sitting on the remaining sheets and I was absolutely one hundred percent correct that there was a very large and pale snake there, all coiled up, but for its head, which was not coiled up but instead lifted from its coil and facing me with the anguished look of a creature rudely awakened.

I stood very still and held the sheet. The snake made wavy snake moves with its head but remained otherwise still.

We stood off.

I have said already that I can win any such standoff and this particular circumstance was a case in point.

That is to say, the snake moved first.

The snake uncoiled with surprising dexterity, considering the intricacy of its coiling, and shot across the space between us and flicked my ankle with its angry tongue. And with its angry fangs, I found out soon enough, as I sank to the couch and the snake disappeared beneath it.

An examination of my ankle showed tiny twin teeth marks. I have never understood the logic behind sucking the venom from one's snake wound, as it would seem to me to merely be ingesting the same poison through another equally vulnerable orifice; however, it was an impulse I made every attempt to carry out. Unfortunately, the bite was located on the outside of my ankle, which, if you were to try right now upon your own self, you'd realize is an impossible location on which to fasten one's mouth. I am a flexible being and I was a no less flexible being back then, and I would think that if ever such a contortion could be managed, with the panic and adrenaline it would have been managed at that moment.

Like I said: however.

Et cetera.

I could not reach the outside of my ankle with my lips and then I stopped trying. I tried instead to beat down the door behind which Binelli and The Lamb had disappeared. I used my fists and one shoulder and then the other shoulder and my hips, and I used my freshly rediscovered voice to wake them from the apparent comas into which they had swiftly slipped upon barricading themselves in their fortress. There was no response and it was a very sturdy door. I did it relatively little damage. Relative to the damage incurred upon my aforementioned appendages, that is to say.

And then I lay down on the couch and covered myself with the cool green sheet and prepared to die. It seemed a terrible shame, so soon after recovering my voice, but it was all that was left me. I thought many a regretful thought while I waited, some of which seemed to me quite profound, and I did get up once to write some things down on a pad of paper Binelli had left on the coffee table. On the top of the first page, he had written: *Finley,* and below that: *Russian,* and I left those things there and turned to a fresh sheet and made to write down my final thoughts. But once faced with the paper, all I could manage was: *Bit by snake. Thanks for the tea. Finley.*

I ripped that sheet of paper carefully from the pad, making sure to leave the first intact, though I didn't suppose Binelli would have further need of his notes on me, what with my untimely demise. But one hates to have it said that one's last act was in fact the destruction of another's property. I folded my note and left it sitting on the pad and I lay back down.

# 11

**I woke to Binelli's voice** and, simultaneously, to the sensation of being pinned down by an automobile tire.

The voice was saying, —So I see you've met Lavendar.

The sensation was saying many things all at once but mostly, —You seem to have been pinned down by an automobile tire.

I chose to not open my eyes for a while. I heard domestic sounds: yawning, water flowing from a faucet, paper ripping, a tea kettle's whistle, and so forth. I waited until I smelled the smell of tea close by, and then I opened my eyes.

I was not pinned down by an automobile tire.

I was pinned down by a tremendous coil of snake. The coil was on my stomach, exactly where I would pouch a baby if I were, as they say, With Child, which I thankfully was not. The coil showed both head and tail resting dead center. I wondered how exactly that worked; the coil seemed perfectly wound and not as if the two ends could end up in the same central location. It was extraordinarily heavy and I breathed shallow breaths. This was not from fear. I remembered immediately that the snake had already killed me quite neatly the previous night, so there was nothing more it could do. I pushed against the couch with my feet so I could sit up a little without disturbing the snake. I was not afraid but all the same, you know, I didn't want to wake it up again. Seeing as that was exactly what had raised its ire the night before.

# 12

**About the gravel,** discussed only, if you'll recall, cursorily quite early in the proceedings: It was no joke.

You may likely have thought, then, of the gravel one might find in somebody's driveway in a rural community, or a vacant lot: vague scattered bits of stone, mostly dust really, covering a solid surface.

This gravel was not that gravel.

This gravel seemed to be covering nothing so much as more gravel. I don't know a) how deep it went or b) what was below it, but my guesses would be a) deep and b) as already noted, gravel. Atop more gravel, atop marshland.

That's how it seemed. To walk around atop this gravel was like walking in those dreams one sometimes has, where the walking one does can hardly be called walking at all. Those dreams where one's legs seem to have lost all connection to the previously not-necessary-to-even-think-about-so-automatic-is-it mechanism attaching and co-ordinating the limbs and brain.

Or like how I would imagine it feels to be in one of those huge boxes of balls that they sometimes provide as an amusement for children at carnivals.

I have never, so far as I can surmise, been turned loose in one of those boxes, but I have seen the children wobble about, legs giving way under every step, and so can imagine at any rate the sensation.

There would appear to be nothing amusing about it.

The balls are perhaps less uncomfortable than gravel to thrash about in; nonetheless.

Although children evidently enjoy the chaos of such endeavors. I wonder why. Is it that their lives are generally more ordered than ours—told when to wake, brought to their various appointments and schools and recitals, read aloud to from books of someone else's choosing, put to sleep at the proper times and so forth? Do the children who live less ordered lives perhaps not so much enjoy being plunked into the unstable world of a box of balls? The children of opium addicts, say, or gypsies? It might be something for someone to study sometime, perhaps in a report of their own if they find themselves so inclined; it however is beyond the realm of this particular account, which remains precisely and professionally focused on the matter at hand. I bring up the gravel simply to shed some light on certain realities. For instance: the difficulty we faced on an almost constant basis, in the most basic facet of locomotion; the shortness of temper at times displayed by certain members of our party; the perhaps unduly lethargic pace with which we carried out our Assignments.

But has that light been shed at all? I mean simply to suggest that in a well-ordered existence, one in which the various tasks of the various days are not so various at all but consistent, regulated, one might perchance decide that to dive willingly into a box of balls would be a fine and worthwhile endeavor.

I would not be that one.

I would not willingly dive.

I would not mind, however, getting into some stage-acting. This seems to me to be a perfect blend of the regulated and the chaotic: One is provided with a narrative, some lines of dialogue, some instruction on how to move about within an admittedly confined space among an admittedly limited cast of characters, all the while operating under a small amount of duress and uncertainty as to the outcome. This stage-acting thing, yes, I think I would not so much mind.

Which is, as it turns out, the only light that was needing to be shed in this extended descriptive passage, although I have perhaps managed to ink in the landscape a bit, which could certainly come in handy. At some point. For someone.

# 13

Wherever we went, wherever the concerns in need of Investigation took us, we always stayed at Tiki Ty's Tiki Barn. And unlikely seeming as it seems, it always seemed to be exactly the same place.

One learns that certain questions are unanswerable.

This is why we need words like 'conundrum.'

Tiki Ty's was always where we stayed and was always a large bright generous sort of bookstore-slash-vintage surfing memorabilia museum. The books were not necessarily about vintage surfing memorabilia; I perhaps misspoke. There were few, if in fact any, books on vintage surfing memorabilia at Tiki Ty's and perhaps in the whole of the world. Vintage surfing memorabilia being one of those memorabilias that people prefer to see accidentally or even on purpose, in person, but rarely, if ever, to read about.

Though perhaps they would enjoy a picture book of vintage surfing memorabilia?

This may not even be the case.

This may be something that warrants further investigation, but perhaps by someone else.

Tiki Ty was always expecting us, though I never saw anyone send a messenger ahead, and always had the same small rooms available for our use whenever we arrived. Tiki Ty always greeted us with a happy good nature that we without fail found vaguely alarming and suspicious at first, and then warmed up to. Tiki Ty had great massive waves of jet black hair that he piled always into a large artistic clump on the top of his head and fixed in place with an invisible elastic band and then a profoundly visible enameled stick, perhaps the length of a schoolchild's straight-edge. Tiki Ty served shrimp in an unusual way, which is to say, not fresh and pink and pearly but battered and cooked and spiced in a manner that I would not have thought of and indeed never thought of at all outside of Tiki Ty's immediate presence but which all the same made my mouth water in a Pavlovian sort of anticipation each and every time I entered the Tiki Barn.

My mouth watered in a Pavlovian sort of anticipation. Tiki Ty greeted us in a riot of black hair and pale green scrubbish garb and shuffling holey mules made of balsa or seagrass or salsa.

No.

This last is incorrect.

However.

He greeted us also with shrimp, arrayed around a puddle of dipping on a large metal platter that once had a painted spray of peonies featured beneath the shrimps but that now with time and with use had faded to only the idea of peonies.

*Raffia.*

Tiki Ty uses a different sort of dipping as well. His dipping is not red but yellow, and not spicy but quiet and like an animal.

# 14

We had been at the Tiki Barn not long enough to make even a dent in even the initial welcoming platter of shrimps when she came in through the bathroom window!

She did not. That was a terrible and willful untruth. Only it has a certain ring to it, doesn't it, a ring that could be put to musical accompaniment and made into a popular song, no? She came in through the bathroom window!

But she did not.

She came scraping in through a window, yes, but not a window living in the bathroom, no, nothing so catchy as that for Kiki B, whose name for purposes of clarity I reveal at this juncture of the account but which of course I couldn't have known at the time. She scraped pathetically in through the bright oversized window of the stockroom—a window one might not even notice, even as it sat there so oversized and bright, for the reason that the stockroom was piled high, high, high to the ceiling with books and vintage surfing memorabilia.

She upset a great many things, entering.

She made, one could say, an entrance.

Kiki B was of an aspect no pleasanter than that of me. Perhaps far worse. In that she was, for one, entirely and generously naked.

Generously not in that there was a generous much of her, but generous in that the nakedness was complete, almost complete, complete but for a jangling sort of wristlet made of bright blue beads and some gold hanging things.

Other than the wristlet, her nakedness was complete. Generous. We averted our eyes.

She cleared her throat.

We kept our eyes averted.

She cleared her throat again, adding this time drama and insistence. She coughed several times in a delicate manner and then several more times in a manner not delicate but one might say tubercular, and then—and this was the point at which we could no longer keep our eyes averted—she barked.

—Bless you, said The Lamb.

—Thank you, said Kiki B.

There was then awkward silence until another pile of books and vintage surfing memorabilia lost its valorous battle with gravity and fell. It'd been trying, trembling, since Kiki B's entrance to remain upright, but as no one was paying any attention, anyhow, it succumbed. To gravity. And to its own vanity, one must assume, as a collective of objects accustomed to being observed, and handled, and commented upon.

We all ignored the poor forgotten objects, now without even their pride, heaped so unceremoniously there on the dusty stockroom floor, and stared instead at Kiki B.

The Lamb stared at the legs, perhaps at the knees. Likely at the knees. The Lamb has hateful knees and thus uses the knees to size up new people.

Murphy stared at the wristlet, perhaps gone agog at the sight of a shiny thing.

Binelli stared at the feet, and then at the calves, and then at the knees, then the thighs and et cetera. He started from the bottom and stared all the way up to the very top, and then glanced quickly at me and then the others and then right back again to the top, from which point he stared from top to toe and in every and all likelihood back up again.

Tiki Ty stared in a general sort of disinterested way at the whole of Kiki B and then at the mess of his stockroom and then, like Binelli, at the rest of us, quickly and each. Then again at the mess on the floor.

—Why must you always come through that window, he said at last.

—I must, she said. She shrugged without apology. She shook her singularly adorned limb and the beads made a barely audible jangle before settling again about her wrist. The tiny jangle made Murphy jump.

—You upset everything. Tiki Ty's tone was less admonishing than matter-of-fact.

Kiki B did a little sudden dance. —I'm an upsetter! she said. She shimmied to the right. —I couldn't be better! she said. She shimmied to the left.

—Well you couldn't be better at upsetting. He gave her that.

She shook her wristlet triumphantly above her head.

Her head was what I stared at. Personally. Which is a fact I perhaps forgot to include earlier in the staring section. I stared at her head in general and then more specifically at her hair.

What can be said of such hair.

For one, that there was very much of it, an indecent, one could say, amount of hair. For two, it was dirty blond. Not the dirty blond that is a hair color in and of itself: dirtyblond; but rather *blond hair that was dirty*. Perhaps dirtyblond as well, or perhaps just blond, or perhaps something else entirely. It was hard to determine. But filthy and with that piecey aspect hair attains when that hair has gone for a very long time without enjoying the acquaintance of a good boar-bristled brush.

I used my good boar-bristled brush each evening on my own hair. It was, as were all my grooming supplies, Binelli-issued and of the finest quality. Binelli issued my shampoo and conditioning and toothpaste and eyedrops and dry-skin lotion for the face and hands and elbows and feet. All, I have mentioned, of the finest quality.

Binelli concerned himself greatly with quality control.

He found it prudent to make a good impression.

—What, Tiki Ty wondered, —are you doing here.

—I have something for you, said Kiki B, answering Tiki Ty but looking in fact directly at me, which was surprising as I didn't yet even know she was Kiki B nor what being Kiki B might mean for her or for anyone else; this not-knowing despite knowing her already in a practically carnal way.

What with the nakedness.

I looked at the rest of them.

The rest of them shrugged except for Binelli, who was watching Kiki B closely and in a manner that appeared almost coiled to spring.

Where was Lavendar, I was reminded to wonder. Lavendar usually preferred to be where the action was. Lavendar prided himself on remaining up-to-date and in-the-know.

If Lavendar were better connected and in possession, I suppose, of a working pair of hands, Lavendar would have made a fine gossip columnist.

Kiki B felt around her person and then laughed mightily. —But it's in my pocket! she said with what seemed to be triumph but was certainly something else.

Though Kiki B's bar for triumph, for all I knew, might have been set very very low. But so low as to be groping about oneself's naked person, having no, being not of marsupial origin, pockets, and so without even the message with whose safe transfer one was charged?

A very low bar, indeed.

—A lack. Alas! She paused from her singsong and then continued, as if thoughtfully, —Unless I stuck it in my—

—Where's your robe, Tiki Ty said quickly.

—I haven't, she said, —the foggiest.

—Well don't you think you ought to retrieve it.

—They'll be by shortly.

They were. They came in through the bathroom window!

They did not.

I apologize.

They came through the same window Kiki B had. Two of them, dressed each and identically in white nurses' smocks and there the similarity ground down to a nub. One was huge. *Huge.* This I cannot emphasize even close to enough to create the impression of even one half, one quarter, one sixteenth of this being's enormity. I could sit here and say it over and over again, huge, huge, or, for interest, say it different ways, making fine use of the lexicon at my easy disposal: vast, mammoth, massive, colossal, titanic, *gnarly* (the lexicon, I should mention, is a fairly specific volume, geared toward those seeking to expand their wave-riding vocabulary, though I have made it clear that not *all* the books in the bookstore portion of the Tiki Barn are related, necessarily, to the surfing and surfing-memorabilia arts) until the sentiment is bled of all meaning and substance and yet, yet still I could not come even a fraction closer to conveying the sheer enormity of this white-smocked creature.

How had they found enough starched white linen.

—Who are you writing about? The Lamb said, bouncing a bit on her knees like a child. —Who's so obese?

Were other nurses going without?

—Kiki B? Did you think she was so fat? The Lamb's face was inches from my own, beaming.

Was—and here good heavens! I thought, so plowed over by my own Investigative prowess that I flushed just a bit about the apples of my cheeks and the knobs of my collar—Kiki B a defrocked nurse, forced into her otherwise inexplicable nakedness by the breadth and scope of starched white linen required to garb this immense freakish phenomenon of nature at its most awry?

—So freakishly fat? Is that what you wrote?

—Are you reading over my shoulder, I said, turning from my page. —Why are you so close to me.

—You mutter aloud when you write, The Lamb said. She flicked her magnificent hair. —It's a sign of lower intelligence.

She picked herself up from her squat and began flouncing off. —I couldn't care less what's in your stupid report anyway.

The other nurse was quite small and with skin like a raisin.

This other nurse swaddled Kiki B in a robe of fuchsia silk, sprayed with flowers and characters of an eastern persuasion. This other nurse took a wide-toothed comb of bone from a breast pocket of misleading size and with the word BATTERSEA stitched above in neat blue script and began tugging at Kiki B's hair. This other nurse after making a certain amount of headway through the tangle though not quite a lot of headway replaced the wide-toothed bone comb whence it came and took from the same and increasingly magically proportioned breast pocket a large silk flower and clipped it behind Kiki B's left ear, pulling some of the hair back with it.

—There, said this small pruney nurse, looking critically at Kiki B. —There's something.

Kiki B beamed in the manner of children and idiots the world over and pulled from the pocket of her freshly acquired robe a folded piece of paper. She handed it to me.

It was taken from me swiftly. So swiftly that my arm remained awkwardly outstretched for some moments after, fingers pinched around a paper-sized bit of air.

Binelli tucked the scrap into his own breast pocket, which was of the usual size and had no resplendent stitching above.

I moved my arm in as casual a manner as I could manage back to my side, where it hung a touch awkwardly. I made quick shaking movements to exercise the oddness out of it. Limbs should always be made comfortable.

The corner of the paper covered where some stitching would go, if Binelli had had some stitching above his breast pocket.

I thought we should perhaps look into some stitching.

It really was quite distinguished.

Only what would ours say.

It would take some looking into.

—Would you care for some shrimps, said Tiki Ty, quite out of the blue.

—We should be going, the raisiny nurse told him, —but thank you nonetheless.

—Is there. The large nurse looked at the ground shyly. —Is there any way. What I mean to say is, might it be possible—

—Of course, said Tiki Ty jovially. —I'll bag some up for your return trip. I have spill-proof containers for the dipping.

—Bless you, said the nurse. —You are good and you are great.

—And I shall have you on my plate! said Kiki B, beaming a benevolent smile after Tiki Ty's departing backside.

—Is that any way to talk, said the raisin.

—It's one way, said Kiki B in a sulky manner, and then no one spoke until Tiki Ty returned to the room with an enormous vat of shrimps and a spill-proof container filled with dipping.

I worried.

I worried I must admit something awful about our remaining supply of shrimps and dipping. I felt a sudden and blistering annoyance toward not only the huge nurse but for the huge in general, who take far more shrimps than their due.

And seating on the trains. And white linen. And freshwater pearls. Et cetera.

The nurse became almost glazed of eye and aspect. —Bless you. O bless you, Tiki Ty.

The threesome made to take their leave.

Kiki B firmly in tow, the shrimpmonger and the raisin made to heave on and all through the window whence they came. Unfortunately for the future of popular music, not located in the bathroom. Kiki B cast a beatific smile over those of us remaining. It was an exit smile, an Exit, the gracious and munificent queen of a country or pageant sweeping out on the arms of her keepers.

—Wait, Binelli said. He gestured toward the bare feet of Kiki B with something akin to horror.

The feet were certainly scratched and of the bluish hue sometimes favored by vampires or victims of frostbite.

They were certainly filthy.

Kiki B smiled and the nurses made impatient noises.

—Doesn't she have shoes, Binelli said, strangling a little bit.

—It's lucky she got the robe. The shrimpmonger spoke with disdain dripping from that cavernous mouth as so very surely the honey and the crumbs and the pie fillings did with regularity.

The shrimpmonger had certainly undergone a bit of a personality adjustment now that the shrimps had been claimed.

—Well she can't go on without shoes. Binelli had something now akin to hysteria about his eyes.

# 15

**Binelli, it might be useful to mention** at this point in the report, once had a sister. This was a sister who in her short time on this earth approached nothing so much as sainthood. She is certainly a saint now, at least, very much dead and gone as she is. This sister had the unlikely red hair of the devil, but red hair that—as Binelli is quick to point out when the subject arises, which it sometimes does and sometimes doesn't, sometimes doesn't for long stretches of time and then arises several times over the course of a day in rapid succession, and then perhaps might not arise for a month or two or six, even, and then arises and arises until we all wish this sister from high atop the grandest golden throne in whatever afterworld had admitted her would *smite* her brother in some way that would include but not be limited to the removal or crippling of his larynx, or thorax, or other crucial component of the general mouth-to-sternum region of his person where the apparati responsible for his talking are housed—so far surpassed my own red hair in terms of gloss, shine, hue, cascadability, volume, manageability, tossability, length, amplitude, and texture, that one would not even, if one were to see the two of our heads of hair side by side, refer to them both as red. Not even refer to them both as hair.

I cannot tell you what they would refer to the one not referred to as hair as. That will remain a question for the ages.

Ultimately, to get the snow shoveled at least in the general direction of the point for this is not after all a traipse through a meandering wood nor a lark through a bubbling brook but a report, in fact, digressions notwithstanding, Binelli and this sister made shoes. I am absolutely one hundred percent positive that behind this fact is an even longer story of a daddy on the dole or a mother in her cups, some manner of neglect and nursemaids and a kindly old manservant who let them polish the household ones-and-twos, a chore to which they against all odds took a shine and began noticing all the little ways upon which they might improve said shoes et cetera ad nauseum. Whatever the sordid story behind it, Binelli and this sister made shoes. They sketched designs for shoes and gathered the materials for shoes and procured the equipment one might need to put shoes together and even pressed their own leather labels into the soles of these shoes: RUSTY BINELLI. Now was Rusty a childish Binelli-issued nickname for his redheaded sister, or was it a reference to the scavenged nail that poked one or the other young cordwainer in the big toe and began a period of infectious infirmary that would lead to the necessity of finding a crafty activity to fill the long hours of bedridden days, an activity of which the children failed to tire, though strength returned; *no* by god, they never tired of this, the smell of leather, the meticulous stitching, the shodding of the people, the heady glamour, the creative juices stirring within pent-up loins, loins that hungered for the tickle of a stray red wisp tossed carelessly past a hollowed cheek—well, it is all conjecture and as such not for this report to contemplate. Shoes were made, many shoes. All women's, only one pair of each style, and without exception every single one a clownish, nay *freakish,* size 9.5. All of which—but for a select and ever-rotating assortment Binelli trundled about in a battered valise like a sole-struck huckster—are housed in a room back at the main place, brown boxes stacked to the ceiling, like some sort of morgue or fallout shelter.

They are, I willingly admit, spectacular.

They are also an unending source of pain and fury for myself and The Lamb. We are neither of us even close to a size 9.5. Who is. A penguin. A clubfoot. A saintly redheaded sister with no need for shoes, not ever again, wafting about the clouds in her wherewithal, no doubt, in her birthday suit, in the buff, with specially made size 9.5 wings erupting from giant shoulder blades to carry her wherever she might deign to go. An entire room filled with handcrafted, timeless, *useless* shoes.

One could go mad.

One does go mad, often, and then the other one, and then both for some time, and then some shoes get thrown about and the memory of the sister desecrated and defamed and then all are yelled at and then all get crappy Assignments next time around.

# 16

Such as Puppets.

# 17

**Dame Uppal and I sat** in an easy silence for some time. A strangely easy silence, one might say, since we were unacquainted each with the other and such situations generally require a trying. A terse semblance of small talk, say, or a forced exchange of compliments.

She was hard to compliment.

Although her dressing gown was splendid.

Her dressing gown was, in fact, a thing that might well have been crafted by fairies, if fairies existed. It was of a color somewhere between cream and raspberry, with not enough on either side to definitively place it in either camp, and shot through with fine threads of gold. The finest, so fine indeed that it took careful scrutiny to even locate these threads and recognize them as such and not just attribute the overall golden aspect to a heavenly glow emanating from within.

Or without, either way.

If heaven existed.

Then, upon the hue and the golden aspect, a fading plum riot of orchids.

It was a fine thing beneath which lay, like something beached, a decidedly un-fine creature.

—It's a lovely dressing gown, I said.

—It's a lovely day, she parried.

It was not a lovely day, but I played along. —It's a lovely home.

—It's a lovely hair, she said, and she gestured awkwardly toward my head.

It seemed a bit of a low blow. It seemed as though only one of us was being earnest in the conversation. It *was* a lovely dressing gown, and home, if one cared for the baroque style.

We lapsed into a silence somewhat less easy.

I would not so much have minded a nibble on some meats.

The other Uppal entered the room at last, sans meats but full of bluster and nerves.

—You've been well entertained I hope, he said with an apologetic gesture toward his mate.

Dame Uppal deigned to move her head ever so slightly in the direction of his voice.

—You've been fed I hope, he said hopefully. —Sated on cured meats and the like?

—I have not. I glared in a reproachful manner toward Dame Uppal, our easy companionship torn asunder by her mocking of my hair.

The hair, I perhaps have already mentioned, is not my fault.

—O dear then. Professor Uppal looked with dismay at his heap on the divan, and then shook his head briskly. —O dear. Well, we shall have to do something. Won't you come to my study.

Dame Uppal ignored our exodus, letting instead her chin drop to rest on her sternum. She was perhaps admiring her dressing gown, admittedly still quite fine.

I followed the Professor down a hallway lined with tapestries that looked to be of medieval provenance, though quite neatly preserved to maintain their rusty patina. I would not personally have chosen the overall palette, finding umbers and crimsons and muddy browns a bit heavy and claustrophobic, but I could not argue with the quality of the decorating, nor of the consistency of tone and mood.

The study supported this observation. It was a study that might

have been featured in a periodical dedicated to the study of studies, so studious was its bearing. It had the dark wood, the saturated
rugs, the floor-to-ceiling bookcases and the heavy oak desk indica-
tive of serious contemplation, meticulous research, and philosoph-
ical argument.

Indeed, there was a marbled chess set upon an equally marbled pedestal, with the pieces either intentionally or organically ar-
ranged in demonstration of a quite elaborate sequence.

Someone had just castled queenside.

The Professor settled into his leather chair with an aspect of
heaviness his physical form neither espoused nor required. Such
heaviness in color, alas! It can change a man.

—My wife, he said. —Please understand—

—Was there talk of meats? I cut him off. My temper was un-
well, and I cared not for his explanations.

—Yes, yes very well. He understood I'd had a trying spell out in
the sitting room. He understood that a tray of cured meats might
set me to rights. He cried out, quite suddenly, but firmly, —Odille!
and barely a moment had passed before a door in the bookshelves
that I had certainly not noticed though my noticing skills have
always been quite exemplary opened inward and into my vision
stepped a Vision.

# 18

**To describe Odille** is a trying matter.

I might begin thus with a small but important reminder: Clichés were at one time not clichés. They were descriptions. Overuse wrested their aptness right from them, apt as they might yet be, and one no longer feels entitled to say: Her eyes were the ink of the night sky, twinkling with stars.

However.

Her eyes were the ink of the night sky, twinkling with stars.

Her hair shone like wet tar, ravenblack. Her figure was an hourglass. Her skin was like finely ground cacao beans, with roses in her cheeks painted on as if with the finest grade of paint, with the finest grade of brush.

Et cetera.

She was tragic. In any film, in any play, in any long torrid romantic novel, Odille would be killed quite unfairly, two thirds of the way through, her soul to the end as light as her eyes were dark. I felt almost sorry for her with that thought: poor innocent, struck down by an ugly world for the unforgivable offense of burning so brightly. I looked sympathetically at her. I smiled.

She looked concerned. —Are you all right, she said, and at the sound of her voice all sorry-feeling and benevolence ended.

Her voice was like a thousand nightingales, singing at sunset. At twilight? At just-dusk?

Whenever nightingales do happen to sing, at any rate, they make a sound like the voice that poured from her lips, stained a childish red and perfectly formed, like twin—

—Is she all right.

My eyes had fluttered shut for just a second. I was upon a veranda, at dusk or sunset or somesuch. Nightingales populating the willow trees. Sheer white curtains billowing in the heavy sea breeze.

—She needs some meats. The Professor snapped his fingers. —Tout de suite.

I came to. My satchel shifted and Odille glanced at it quickly and then slipped right back through the bookshelves, leaving only an intoxicating sort of persimmon smell to prove that she'd been there at all.

# 19

**With Odille and her lusty sway** vanquished from the room and the promise of meats on the horizon, the Professor and I got back to business.

I took a breath. —There was something, then, about Puppets.

The Puppet Man emerged from the bearing of the Professor. His whole face changed shape. It became eager, lost ten to fifteen year's worth of wrinkles and the wisdom anecdotally associated with them. The eyes gleamed, glittered. His cheeks rouged like a showgirl's.

—Yes yes. I admit, I was surprised—pleasantly surprised, yes, so very pleasantly!—when Binelli alerted me to your interest. Your organization's—it's an organization, yes?—interest, indeed, pleasantly, not to assume that you have a personal interest—but you do, don't you, that's why they assigned you, yes?

—Perhaps, I said, holding up a silencing hand, —I should be asking the questions?

The Puppet Man clamped shut his lips like a child but nodded vigorously and made for me an agreeable face.

But for the lips.

They were too full, somehow. All pursed up in that way.

There was a long silence.

I stared at the Puppet Man. What was he trying to pull. We locked eyes, his bright and moronic, mine narrow as Lavendar's.

I cased him.

I waited for him to crack.

He waited for me, I realized suddenly, to ask the questions I'd indicated were stewing in my brain.

Vital questions, yes. For the edification, yes, of the organization.

I don't know what Binelli tells these people.

—Can you, I said, —bring the Puppets out. Slowly.

He nodded, lips still all one smashed into the other like a bloody trainwreck above his chin.

—You can speak, I said. —Please.

—I just get very excited, yes. My family, he waved his hand grandly through the air, as though surrounded by teeming hordes of relations, —they do not understand. Or, they're quite clever, they *understand*, I misspoke. They do not, he groped what might have been Dame Uppal's left breast, if she'd been in the room and standing just so, —care.

His eyes lost none of their luster so I spent not a shred of sympathy on the Puppet Man right then at that moment. Many people care not for many things.

I care not for Puppets, as I've made clear.

I cared not particularly for the Puppet Man either, but in not the same way. In that I had no reason to loathe or fear the Puppet Man.

I had reason to loathe and fear Puppets.

I had reason also no doubt to loathe Russians, but that reason was locked away. The Puppets I remembered. The Puppet encounter from which emerged my loathing toward and fearing of Puppets happened in the stretch of time since I'd emerged from the silence, and for this stretch of time I have an excellent memory.

Elephantine, one could say.

If one were in the habit of comparing persons to pachyderms.

Which I am not.

The Puppet Man directed my attention to what I might have up until then assumed, if I were the assuming type, to be a window, being curtained. Which I am not.

The assuming type. Not curtained.

Which I am not, either.

Neither curtained nor assuming, that is.

Nor unduly suspicious of inanimate objects unless, for instance, those objects are of a sudden *imbued* with animation and grow and contort with a grotesquerie last known in this world during, what, the reign of the gods? So suspicious, yes, but not *unduly* so, when one is walking down a crowded street of a scaffolded town on a Sunday morning, just taking an hour away from focused Investigating to have a bit of air, find a shrimp, get oneself refreshed, and one doesn't right off the bat notice the ropes and pulleys, the teams of struggling Puppet Men trying to keep their unruly charges at bay.

—Are you talking about the Parade again, Murphy said.

—It is difficult, I said, —to write an accurate yet gripping report with the frequent interruptions.

The Puppets had been many in hue and shape and girth and demeanor, similar only in an unwavering maniacal hovering. *Looming.*

—I'm not sure, Murphy said, —that those would even be considered officially Puppets.

Murphy had found me a bit later that particular Sunday morning in an alleyway, sharing a canteen of something resembling hinge-oil with someone who resembled a chimney sweep.

—I was not aware, I said, —that you were here in the capacity of an official representative of the Federation Against the Defamation and/or Misidentification of Puppets. If this is, I said, —indeed the case, might I suggest you write up your own report. We can each be quite silent and write our reports on Investigations and Puppets respectively.

—You're not even writing about the Investigation, Murphy said. He rattled his pockets with great agitation. —That Parade was years ago. You wouldn't even have remembered it if Binelli hadn't assigned you to Puppets.

—I remember, I said, —*everything*, despite the fact of almost constant and purposeless interruption, without which in this case I would have long since finished recounting the fact of Mr.—*Professor*—Uppal's Puppets, which is certainly about this Investigation, presumably the entirety of this Investigation, as you seem to have little enough to do with this Investigation that you're able to spend your time here interrupting me.

—You remember everything, Murphy said, with exaggerated incredulity. —You.

He jangled furiously.

The curtain in question was red, in keeping with the study's overall décor, and there seemed to be light emanating from behind it, in the manner of the outdoors. Even if one were not generally the assuming type, one might very well have, not *assumed*, per se, but *deduced*, in the logical and observant fashion as befits certain logical and observant professions, that the curtain hung before a window that hung before the outdoors. Each keeping the next at bay.

I would not have faulted someone for assuming this, at any rate.

The Puppet Man paused before the curtain.

I blinked, anticipating sun.

Then, with my eyes already streaming anticipatory tears, I pulled a pair of enormous aviator-style sunglasses from an enormous hidden pocket secretly located upon my person and donned them.

Some tears dribbled to my chin.

The Puppet Man gave me a look that wondered if I was quite ready, and though he couldn't see it behind my enormous aviator-style sunglasses, I responded with a look that affirmed yes, I was ready, ready as I'd ever be.

He pulled away the great red curtain.

# 20

**Behind the curtain** was a tiny stage, held up by the sort of stilts that can be found propping up precariously located oceanfront homes. These stilts held up the little stage so that it hovered at about eye level to a grown human being.

I am, despite my countless other shortcomings, a grown human being.

There's that, at least, going for me.

I should clarify the tinyness of the tiny stage. It was tiny in the vertical sense, in that it did not go up very high. But it was in relation to its short vertical stature large in the horizontal sense, in that it had quite a wingspan. It was a tiny town suffering from suburban sprawl. None of the grandeur of cityscapes, no, but a flat wide horizon, accommodating beings who didn't care to feel dwarfed by their architecture and would not so much mind a good brisk stroll in order to locate a shrimp stand.

There was a tiny shrimp stand in a spot just left of center.

Manning the shrimp stand was a tiny shrimp vendor.

The Puppet Man pulled on some fancy metallic gloves that had been blanketing the stage's tiny foreground, and moved his thumb and index finger just slightly.

The tiny shrimp vendor offered me a tiny shrimp as the whole tiny town suddenly awoke and leapt into frenzied life.

Tiny golfing men threw tiny golfing clubs into the trunks of their tiny golfing carts. Tiny impeccably turned-out ladies stirred olives into the first of their, one got the sense, many impeccably made lunchtime martinis and wiped tiny lipstick prints from their tiny martini glasses after each tiny sip. Tiny—quite tiny—children tripped over their tiny but yet still too-big-hand-me-down oxford shoes and landed in tiny squalling snotty heaps on the sidewalks, which were littered here and there with the tiny detritus of the town's tiny population.

It was extraordinary, and not what I had expected. These were not the huge furry impaired beasts I had come to know as Puppets. No. I propped my enormous aviator-style sunglasses atop my head. The light had not been sunlight of course, but only a spotlight from behind the stage, illuminating the town in an early afternoon glow. I would come to know that the spotlight shifted, as slowly as the sun, to grant a daily cycle to the TownsPuppets' days. Seasonal filters would be added and taken away—the bluish metal scrape of winter, a honeyed summer gold. The Puppets turned sometimes their tiny faces up to the light, as if soaking in a ray of warmth, or questioning their artificial heavens.

I must have beamed. The Puppet Man's face broke open like an egg and he clapped his gloved hands twice in glee. Several tiny car wrecks resulted. He turned quickly his attentions to the stage and cried, —O no, Odille! and pointed a finger toward a prone pedestrian, ungracefully sprawled in a crosswalk, skirt bunched up around her thighs and a tiny silver platter of meats upset all around her.

—What is it? I was stunned to hear the miniature ask, in the same gale voice as Odille the Larger. I was even more stunned to smell persimmon, and understood that more than I'd even realized once the curtain was first drawn, I was in the presence of something quite enormous.

That something quite enormous, however, was in fact the real Odille, entering the study behind us. Compared to the tiny disheveled Odille, the real Odille seemed suddenly ungainly, almost obscene. Her huge garish lips, identical I noted with the slightest touch of smugness to the Puppet Man's, pursed as she saw her tiny counterpart's countenance.

—Geez, Dad, she said. —I'm no Bolshoi baby, but give me some semblance of grace.

She swept the chess pieces unceremoniously onto the carpet and set the silver tray on the chessboard.

The Puppet Man ripped off his gloves and became once again the Professor. —I remember where I had you, Odille, he said. He pointed at the scattered chessmen. —My rook. Your queen. Et cetera.

—I don't remember that at all, *Professor,* Odille said. She smiled up at him charmingly. —We'll have to start over.

—We can start as many times as you please, dear sweet. Your queen gets it every time.

—My queen, Odille said, —has been taking tango classes. She may yet surprise you.

—She has some new moves then? In her old tired arsenal? The Professor plucked a toothpick from the tray and sniffed at the speared meat. —Mortadella?

—*De notta,* Odille said, and they laughed mightily then, at what sort of private infantile joke I'm sure I had no idea. She turned to me, and I put my enormous aviator-style sunglasses back over my eyes. I felt displeased and out-of-sorts, and her radiance was also blinding.

She did not take the hint.

—So the Professor's been showing you his toys then, she said. —His little dolls. Can you imagine.

She gave me what she must have thought was a conspiratorial smile and I fixed her with my most acerbic glare, although of course she couldn't tell, what with the sunglasses. She winked.

O the twinkle!

I wept a little.

The Professor licked his glistening lips. —Have some meats, he told me. —The finest in season. A lovely plate, don't you think. Odille, your charms have spilled over at long last to the kitchen.

—Mother helped, Odille said.

The Professor and I ignored the blatant untruth and the blatant untruthteller both.

—Would you care for some sake, the Professor instead said.

—I do not care for sake, I told him.

This was a statement I had no hard evidence to support, but for some reason sake was a spirit I distrusted, though I am quite fond of the Japanese people and have found my dealings with them to be always exceedingly civilized.

—You know what, the Professor said, seeming relieved, —I do not care for sake myself. And yet sake I drink, always, ad nauseum, whenever I entertain in my study! How about that!

—Sake is a sorry excuse for a cocktail, Odille agreed.

—Sake is sticky! and sickly! the Professor pronounced gamely, forgetting Odille's minxy lying ways.

—Sake is strictly prohibited! Odille declared.

It was a madhouse. They tore off the doors to the liquor cabinet and flung bottles to the floor. There being rugs, some bottles broke and some didn't. Those that didn't, they picked up again and flung against the walls, where they one by one smashed in a smashing fireworks display of glass and alcohol, leaving bold Rorschach tests of wet against the paint.

One, in particular, resembled a popular landmark in France, but before I could point it out, another bottle smashed right above it, ruining the effect altogether.

I felt I should take my leave.

The meats, however, beckoned aromatically from their tray.

I saw Lavendar poke his head out from the folds of his satchel, grumpily. He glanced about at the ensuing madness and met my eyes with a woebegone look. Where, he was likely wondering, have you brought me and why.

Lavendar generally has a terrible disadvantage in times of sudden disarray, being wrapped up in his satchel and unaware of the leading-up-to moments. He awakes blinking into the garish results, the crescendos, and is forced to shake off his grog all too suddenly and uncoil in a distinctly unleisurely fashion and assess the situation in a heartbeat and spring into action.

Lavendar can uncoil quite quickly.

Lavendar can also, if necessary, leap.

Lavendar leapt from his satchel and made a wild beeline for the still-cracked secret door in the bookshelves, through which he, without even a glance back at me, disappeared in a flash of scales.

Lavendar's love for me knows no bounds but he could take a few lessons in loyalty.

His escape did make an impression upon the company. The Professor and Odille both halted, one in midthrow and the other midbend, and stared after the departed Lavendar.

—Mother, Odille mentioned, —will not be pleased.

We were all then silent.

I know I was and I would imagine they too were awaiting the scream that usually follows one of Lavendar's ill-timed exits.

And yes, there it was.

A fine one too. Full-bodied, with a woody aspect and admirably robust bouquet.

# 21

**Something people don't understand** about snakes, something that makes them think it useful to run all about either after or away from a snake, something that would save those who encounter snakes so much time and effort and construction work on their homes and gardens, is that snakes always come back.

If back is where the snake wants to be.

If the snake would prefer to be somewhere else, then you just have to let that snake go.

But Lavendar is of no concern as regards that matter. Lavendar always returns to me. He takes his time, sometimes, depending on his reasons for going in the first place, but he can always be expected back, at his leisure.

I was thus the only one unconcerned at the Uppal home for the remainder of the afternoon.

# 22

**It would be prudent** here to explain my relationship with Lavendar.

After waking up with the snake I came to know as Lavendar pinning me to the couch like nothing so much as an automobile tire, many things started. Some of the things were and remain quite complicated. Others are simple. One such thing is my relationship with Lavendar.

Lavendar loves me.

As I have previously stated, Lavendar's love for me knows no bounds.

After biting me and sleeping on me, all coiled up on my stomach for an entire night, Lavendar changed his tune. He altered his evidently unfavorable original assessment of my character and bearing and became quite swoony toward me.

For instance: I shifted slightly under his weight, there on the couch, as Binelli and I spoke. I tried to do it so the snake would hardly notice, so he wouldn't feel even remotely perturbed or inconvenienced in the least. But there was one vital organ at the point of bursting its toxins throughout my entire being, and I felt if only I could shift ever so slightly, ever so slowly, I might relieve the pressure without bothering Lavendar.

I shifted gently.

Lavendar looked at me then, with a look I had certainly never seen on a snake but have with equal certainty seen countless times since. This was a look of first almost lazy-eyed confusion. Lavendar looked like a child recently kicked by a mule. This look was followed quickly with a look a bit larger, a bit more comprehending. If ever I had experienced another creature, reptilian or otherwise, shooting me that sort of look, I obviously cannot and did not then, it being so soon after the silence, remember. But the look, it turned out, was the look of a creature completely, helplessly, and tragically besotted.

And then, it was almost as though he was asking me what I wanted. Why the shift? his tiny eyes pleaded. Do you not then love me too?

I shifted again, tentatively.

Lavendar immediately reproportioned his entire self. He uncoiled slowly, almost gently, with such control, and then, with heartbreaking care, slid right up next to me, between my prone body and the back of the couch, so that we lay side by side, his chilled skin barely grazing mine.

What Lavendar did was cuddle me.

We all watched, completely silent, as the entire process unfolded. Uncoiled, as it were. And then, once Lavendar had settled in, once he'd made it quite known how things would be henceforth, Binelli waited for one extra beat before resuming the conversation that would start most of the many many other more complicated things I mentioned earlier.

And Lavendar became my beast of burden.

# 23

**The Lamb and Tiki Ty and Murphy and I** all sat around watching Lavendar.

Lavendar and his kitten-shaped tumor.

Poor miserable Lavendar.

We, at least, were miserable watching Lavendar. Lavendar could very possibly have been in no discomfort whatsoever, and, even more possibly, terrifically pleased.

He had had a fine lunch, after all.

Watching, however, a kitten pass through a snake is not for the faint of heart.

Murphy turned away first.

—Where did he find a kitten, Murphy said.

—On the Assignment, I said. I felt exceedingly downcast about the sequence of events, the longer they'd had to unfold in my mind.

—Binelli won't be happy, The Lamb said, unnecessarily.

—Does Binelli, I said, —really need to find out.

—Binelli finds out everything, The Lamb said, again unnecessarily, and this time with a touch of smug.

I wished The Lamb would be silent.

—Whose kitten was it, Murphy said.

—Odille's. The Puppet Man's daughter's.

The Lamb opened her mouth to offer a new and insightful unnecessary comment but closed it again. It was so unnecessary a comment, evidently, that even she, with her uncanny penchant for such unnecessarities, couldn't be bothered.

—Is this daughter a very young daughter, Tiki Ty said. —Was there crying.

—No, I said. —But yes.

There had been crying.

After the screaming, and then the fruitless hunting, during which time I had sat quietly in the Professor's study, eating of the assortment of meats, there was indeed crying. Crying first of the shaking, finger-pointing, name-calling-through-a-mighty-veil-of-tears variety, and then butcher-knife-waving, kitten-rescuing/vengeance-swearing crying, then finally, relieved-of-weaponry-and-with-it-all-hope, bent-over, quiet crying.

Which was the point at which I had finally been able to seal Lavendar back up in his satchel and take my leave of the Uppal houschold.

The kitten was starting to less resemble itself alive. Still not something you'd want traveling through you, particularly if your diameter was a scant few inches, but Lavendar bore it bravely.

—It was funny though, I said. —The wife, the mother, came into the study during the whole thing, and she seemed just fine. I mean, not at all fine, I said, —in that a snake was loose in her home and she was shrieking and flailing and casting her eyes about wildly, and then of course not fine in that the snake had eaten the family pet, but, well, much finer than she'd been in the sitting room—

—This is not at all interesting, said The Lamb.

The Lamb is, I have perhaps not adequately or at all explained, easily bored. Easy boredom is often attributed to freakish intelligence. But whence The Lamb's freakish intelligence?

One could wonder.

I, being one, have a few theories.

None of which can be proved. When one is one with no recollection of one's past, one does not often inspire full disclosure from others. There evidently is required, for full disclosure, some manner of reciprocity on the part of all parties involved, a reciprocity I am obviously unable to offer.

Proved or no, I have a few theories.

# 24

**Theory No. 1 Regarding The Lamb's Freakish Intelligence:**

The Lamb was born the miserably precocious bastard child of a French prostitute and an equally French taxicab driver. The taxicab driver would regularly bring the prostitute after her dates back to the hovel she shared with three other very French prostitutes, located down the very end of a seedy Marseilles ally. This taxicab driver never requested his due fare for these trips; rather, once a month, he would be invited inside for a 'quadruple bypass'—his affectionate term for the monthly bacchanal to which he was treated by the four prostitute roommates.

The taxicab driver had been led to believe by his beautifully sullen Italian wife that he was incapable of impregnating a lady. On this charge, he was subjected to endless streams of Italian abuse, of whose nature he could only guess, never having studied his wife's native language, preferring instead the romantic fantasy of a foreign tongue in his home and in his ear. While he wasn't so stupid as to suppose she sang nothing but his praises on the telephone to her mother and innumerable sisters back in Milan, he enjoyed writing his own subtitles to these overheard conversations in his head. *He's a tiger in bed,* he imagined the peculiar mix of syllables revealing proudly to jealous relatives and acquaintances. *So strong, so passionate. If I weren't so jealous of every eye in every head of every female who catches sight of him, I'd let you all have a go with him, just to experience for a single night love as it was intended by God in Heaven,* whereupon she'd pantomime the sign of the cross by rote.

Of course, his inability to fill this wife's womb with the child she so fiercely longed to bear eventually led to his being barred from the marital bed. *The sacrifice,* he imagined her telling her mother and sisters ruefully, *is all mine. I had to insist he sleep on the daybed just to quell the desires that threaten to overtake my better judgment when he's beside me. But I want his seed to grow strong and plentiful—and then, o and then, what times we shall have!*

He didn't know how long it would take for his seed to strengthen, but he considered carefully that when the blessed occasion when his wife deemed him fit for further attempts at reproduction arrived, he didn't want old, pent-up seed to constitute his contribution. A monthly deposit, a check to keep the bill collectors at bay, a tithe so to speak—this was all he thought of his quadruple bypasses. And four ladies—never mind their profession, these were ladies—who offered up free what others had to sign over entire paychecks for, well, it kept the old juices flowing what would otherwise—and he didn't know for sure the physiology of it, but he suspected it could happen—dry out from neglect.

What he didn't know, and what the four prostitutes didn't know, was that it was his wife's womb that was barren; his own earnest swimmers had been dejected and rejected for years. In the same month—it had been a low full orange moon the night of the bypass—all four prostitutes came up empty at their time. All four prostitutes bloated and vomited and swelled at all ends, and all four prostitutes had to stop working, hugely pregnant, for one month before and one month following their giving almost simultaneous birth to four enormous girl-children.

One of these girl-children was The Lamb.

The daughters were too many and too huge to keep, realistically. The taxicab driver was terribly sorry for this; he would have been ecstatic to bring his brood home all at once and the prostitutes too, and brag over the most expensive ales and cigars at the corner café about his little ladies and their various sizes and colors and musical screeches. But while he never tested his theory, he suspected that he and his entourage of eight would have no home upon which to joyously descend if word got back to the real Little Lady about what turned out to be his astounding prowess; and he imagined his wife's chagrin when she realized it was she, not he, who kept their bassinette empty and their bloodline short. He vowed she would never know; he consulted instead a doctor who understood all manner of lady trouble and came up with a scheme whereby he could secretly feed his wife prescribed antidotes to her barrenness, mashed up in her evening scotch and soda—a scheme that led at long last to their welcoming a sickly son into their home whose whimpers acted as an unlikely aphrodisiac on his wife and solved for good their stalled romance.

The prostitutes did not believe so much in romance. They instead were worshippers at the altar of commerce, and the math of keeping and providing for four girl-children just did not make good sense, although they did consider the long-term cost-benefit analysis of the automatic inheritance by their daughters of their clientele and how they could possibly all retire early and enjoy a long and well-appointed old age, daughters aplenty bringing in the francs and sending their long-suffering mothers on sightseeing trips and lavish shopping expeditions. But the diapers, the milks, the incomes lost by even a rotating system of caretaking, and all this on top of the months losing and then regaining their working figures—it just wasn't feasible.

They brought the daughters to the Convent of the Blessed Assumption in the dead of a hot August night and scurried away, lighter already and thirsting for four free drinks from four lucky lads who for the right price would have their nights made and made again.

Now the prostitutes had assumed that the convent, this convent, any convent, would care for the girl-babies until such a time as they could each be placed in a good home, with a good family. Not ardent churchgoers, the prostitutes were completely unaware of the dire situation of the Convent of the Blessed Assumption.

The dire situation was such: No one anymore had the slightest desire to devote one's young robust life to God. There weren't so many takers at that particular period for the holey wounded hand of Jesus in matrimony. His star had faded, like those of so many icons before him, and the daughters of Marseilles aimed instead for the heady glamour of a life of prostitution. Gone were the prim virgins and their clicking rosary beads, worn smooth by the worrying of ferocious virginal fingers. Gone were the modest shawls and the pure white dresses, unbesmirched by lust or charcoal wickedness. The prostitutes, understand, of Marseilles were of such quality, of such brimming vigor and vim, such lovely specimens with such lovely charms hidden beneath their colorful scandalous silken wisps, that the cloistered life of the nunnery—the heavy dark worsted capes and the sheer *uselessness* of having to keep all the new rage of haircuts sweeping Provence hidden beneath sackcloth veils—seemed a stupid futile waste of one's girlhood. One could, the girls of Marseilles were realizing, be a savvy independent lady, with the sparkling drinks and dazzling wiles, without entering into a loveless matrimony with Christ and letting one's unfortunately inherited *moustache* enjoy free reign over one's upper lip.

So when the four daughters of the four prostitutes were discovered on the doorstep that sweltering August morning, Sister Michael-Gabriela of Blessed Assumption fell to her knees and wept. A miracle, *a miracle* were the magic words that swept through the cloister, the magic words to describe the magical babies who would ensure the convent's future.

Thus, no adoptions. No globe-trotting families with scads of money yet a lamentable dearth of children would choose a rosy-cheeked bastard to bestow with culture and undeserved inheritance. It was for the girls instead the impoverished life of God's child-brides, and not a spot of even rouge or lip balm to brighten their depressing days.

For the Convent of the Blessed Assumption was not a joyous place. The Sisters would argue that they spent each and every moment in joyous celebration, but their manner of celebration was understated and, as a rule, not even demonstrated with beatific glows shining across their broad wan faces but with a sort of grimness, a furrowed stern determination to Serve and ask nothing in return.

The daughters, who knew no better, who had never been privy to any other form of existence, must have had coded within the very fibers of their collective being a sense that something was awry, because the daughters, to the last, were dreadfully pissed off. These daughters, who had never heard a word against God except perhaps in their first few weeks of life in their mothers' hovel, rolled their eyes at one another in mock dramatic death throes, and mouthed to one another under a strict code of silence their aggravation with the life they'd been unwittingly dealt. And one day, during the daily contemplative gardening hour, one of the four turned to her three miserable compatriots and said, quite out loud, —I'm just so goddamn *bored*.

It was as though an air-raid siren had sounded throughout the convent.

The child had not only damned God, but spoken.

And how had she learned the word.

The girls were separated for the first time since well before birth, as they had in fact all come from the same little sac hanging from the same little man and had spent barely a moment apart since, notwithstanding their nine-month internments in separate wombs. They were separated so the bad seed among them could be ferreted out, so the infection could be contained before it spread through the convent, the last bastion of contagion-free air in all of dirty Marseilles.

The infection was the Devil. It was living in The Lamb.

The other girls could hear the exorcism attempts from their attic-most chamber. They could hear the chanting, the praying, the splashing. They heard rattling and shrieking and most of all, laughing, for The Lamb was finally having some fun. It was a diversion the likes of which she'd never known, a grand break in the daily monotony that her each and every sense was gratefully soaking up like a dehydrated kidney. The sheer volume of the exorcisms, the sounds of the various voices of the Sisters, voices she'd never heard and never even been able to really imagine—this filled her with more glee than she'd known in all her years. Sister Michael-Gabriela, for instance, had the voice of not a man at all, as The Lamb had always supposed, but rather the twang of an American debutante. And when she stood above The Lamb and in all seriousness beseeched please the Devil to vacate, the sound was so unexpected The Lamb almost fell from the bed in hysterics.

She tried out her own voice, all kinds of tones. She spoke from deep within and from the tip of her nose, and she said words she'd only heard whispered aloud. Mostly she said, —It's just so goddamn boring, because it had been these words that had started what she was coming to think of as her new life and she didn't want things to go back anytime soon. She'd been quietly soaking up books and thoughts and silence for so long that her head was ready to explode if some of it couldn't find its way back out into the air around her head, where it could bounce around, off walls, and change itself in its travels to return to her replenished.

And so she was deemed damned. Poor damned Lamb. The Devil had his grips on her good, and to keep her would only lead to the resumed downfall of the Convent of the Blessed Assumption.

One would be sacrificed for the greater Good.

She was turned out onto the doorstep whence she had arrived, in a makeshift tunic sewn from her habit and with only her fiercely brewing brains and a thermos of souring milk to her name.

She dispensed with the milk on the third step, feeling her brains quite enough.

# 25

Thus, **The Lamb yawned mightily** at my story and rolled her eyes.

But it *was* interesting, the more I thought about Dame Uppal's transformation. Which I hadn't had much opportunity to do, back at the Uppal estate, what with the screaming and the running around and the aforementioned stages of grief going on all around me. I had during that time of course maintained steely control of my surroundings, my crack observation mechanism ticking away even as the observations grew surreal and chaotic—such is my training—and I had ferreted these observations away like so many sustaining acorns for a later time.

It was winter. Time to break open the stockpile.

If ferrets in fact act like squirrels. Which I admit I'm not sure about.

I do know that Lavendar wouldn't think twice about eating either one.

In any case. The Dame Uppal who had entered the study, arms flailing wildly and eyes darting across the floor, was a far far cry from the Dame Uppal with whom I'd spoken in the sitting room. The Dame Uppal who flailed and screamed was clearly, for one, upright. She did not wear a dressing gown—that lovely, lovely gown—only half belted and showing far too much leg for a woman of a certain age. This Dame Uppal wore a smart sari set, in a bold marigold hue, and this Dame Uppal had hair intricately plaited and bunned and pinned, not fetchingly disheveled about her shoulders and head at all.

The hair alone should have given me pause. Though in my defense, the hair did start to shake loose, just a bit, over the course of the events that followed. But a hair like that, it doesn't happen in minutes. The most expert bunner cannot take the hair on Dame Uppal from the Sitting Room and transform it to the hair of flailing Dame Uppal of the Study in a matter of minutes. Even taking a vigorous brush to the Sitting Room Dame would have taken too long.

I know about brushing.

Plaiting and bunning and pinning I leave to the professionals and beauty queens, but I do the brushing, tears seeping from my eyes, every night.

And then something even odder had happened. Dame Uppal— the sheveled version—had asked me, even as her daughter was suffering the unholy stages of grief there before us, how had I liked the plated meats she'd prepared.

*She'd* prepared.

I had assumed—not *assumed*.

I had calculated, using a good logical system of inferences, that Odille had prepared the tray of meats. Odille had entered the room, heard our request for sustenance, withdrawn from the room, taken the appropriate amount of time for gathering and setting out in an attractive fashion meats, and borne those meats aloft back to the room where the Professor and I were waiting. I had been in the room only for a short while before Odille's entrance, and the preparation of meats occurred just after that. All to explain, then, the logical system of inferences upon which I had relied—and relied to fine result, historically—to conclude that it had been Odille whose sumptuous feast of plated meats we'd enjoyed, not Dame Uppal's, who'd been in no condition to prepare a sumptuous feast of anything except perhaps an assortment of leftover medications. Which my logical system of inference would then have said must consist of stimulants, she having consumed already all of the available seda-tives, from the look of her, prior to my arrival at the Uppal estate.

So how had Dame Uppal so quickly transformed from the divan diva I'd originally met into the sunny-clothed tidy-bunned mistress of meats I was met with so soon after.

How indeed.

I would need to make another visit. It was quite possible I'd stum-bled upon something more than Puppets in this Assignment, but I would have to be sure. It was quite possible that the Assignment itself was less about Puppets than about this something more I'd uncovered. It was quite possible that I was being tested as to my acuity and acumen and alacrity in digging far beneath the sur-face of an Assignment, right into its seedy underbelly, and slash-ing that underbelly open and revealing a Pandora's box of deceit and corruption.

Lavendar's underbelly, incidentally, bore the imprint of a tiny paw, with its four tiny pads, and I was momentarily touched.

I shook it off, however. I was quite possibly being groomed for promotion within the organization, a promotion entirely depen-dent upon my handling of this Assignment.

I determined to proceed with all due diligence. Right after Lavendar passed the bones.

Murphy jangled his pockets and grimaced throughout.

# 26

**Murphy's marbles were many in color** and rattled in an unsavory way about his head and pockets. Many in number as well. When they spilled, which they did, often and obviously, they made delightful confections on the floor. They mostly spilled in the Tiki Barn. That's when they spilled best and most often and obviously, and most delightfully in that the colors rolled around the brown wooden floors.

Brown wood matches everything, and makes everything around it and upon it brighter and more delightful.

The less delightful aspect of Murphy's frequent and distracting spills was the noise. Hence, 'distracting.' The clatter of Murphy's marbles upon the hardwood of the Tiki Barn floors made everyone startle, not the least of whom was Lavendar.

Startling Lavendar guarantees certain doom. A startled Lavendar would prefer nothing so much as to find the nearest warm body and squeeze the warmth right out of it. Lavendar is mightily soothed by cold flesh. The drawbacks of a startled Lavendar far outweigh the delights of many-colored marbles upon a hardwood floor.

Yellow matches barely anything.

Each time Murphy spilled his marbles I would feel equal parts grateful and furious. And then slight pity toward Murphy for my fury. And then slight fury toward Murphy for the squeezing. Slight annoyance toward Lavendar for squeezing so tight. Slight pity toward Lavendar for my annoyance. Et cetera.

That is then to say: Murphy's marbles were a constant source of internal conflict.

# 27

**I'd indeed had it up to here** with Murphy and his marbles, and quite up to there with The Lamb's wretched eye rolling, and a rather ugly and prolonged spell of concern with Lavendar's digestive histrionics. The Uppal estate would want inevitably several days to simmer out its aggravation toward my snake and myself before we would once again be welcomed onto the premises, and everyone seemed terribly busy with their Assignments anyhow.

All this to say, when Tiki Ty invited me along for a field trip, I accepted.

We set out to see Kiki B.

Rarely did it happen that I and Tiki Ty found ourselves alone together, and while on the one hand it certainly seemed a treat, a little adventure among friends and neighbors along the winding trails of which we might reveal our innermost selves and peal with laughter and pet in fondness and get serious and somber and clutch and weep, on the other hand it was just this side of awkward.

We were so rarely responsible, either of us, for the entire brunt of conversation.

—Have you taken a lover, I said.

It was perhaps not the correct thing.

—How are the vintage surfing memorabilias selling, I said hurriedly.

I hoped he would address only the second address and chalk up that first to simple miscalculation.

Tiki Ty opened his mouth to speak and quickly, not wanting to take any chances, I said, —Your name and Kiki B's name are quite alike are they not.

There.

I've learned some things about the fine art of conversation. Now he would not possibly address the earliest address, that nonsense and triviality, being far too long in the past, and if he were to in fact scope his mind back a touch, it would alight quite naturally upon the address regarding his work. He had thus a nice choice of springboards from which to bounce, slowly and evenly to get his bearings and then higher and higher until finally, the glorious swan dive into conversation, either practical or abstract, I cared not which.

—How's that, he said.

This was unexpected. His dive into conversation gave no indication as to which prompt he was responding. Which cool clear surface he was aiming to break with his lithe, slippery form.

There is only one way to fight a certain manner of conversationalist.

—How's what, I said.

Up the long ladder again with him, now a mite more tired, the springboard's surface now puddled, but with a rare opportunity to erase his previous, low-scoring attempt at natural after all human interaction.

—How's my name like Kiki B's.

Perfect.

I clapped and held up a victorious 10! I interviewed him for a rapt viewing audience, with him still in his towel and dripping with triumph and chlorine. I placed a medal reverently around his smooth, suntanned neck and positioned it just so. I nodded modestly as he jabbed a finger toward where I stood, just outside the lime-light, that finger indicating he couldn't have done it without me, that a share of that medal and the smooth torso upon which it was positioned just so belonged rightfully to the one who had coached him all this time, through so many setbacks and false starts, who had taken the lumpy raw material with which he was naturally blessed and molded it, lovingly, into the heroic flesh that stood there today.

He gently wrested his arm from my caressing grasp.

He allowed me a moment.

I took gratefully that moment, retracing my steps ever so slowly until I had found my way to an appropriate juncture some way back. I banished metaphor and smooth muscle from my mind.

—Well, I said, —they do, do they not, sound quite alike. Kiki B. Tiki Ty. Don't you hear it.

He shrugged. —I suppose, if you really reach. But don't you hear how hers just keeps shooting in one direction: Kiki B? And mine turns that sharp corner: Tiki *Ty*? And also, how hers is back-ward from mine?

—Backward.

—Well yes, how the *iki* part in hers is actually her, whereas in mine, it's simply descriptive. You see.

—Well of course, I said, though I saw in fact nothing. I wished a little bit that he had gone with the other conversational prompt he had been so generously offered. I was in way over my head. I grasped at straws.

—And don't you know that your name part, the part in yours that's actually you, comes after?

Well that threw him for a loop.

—No, he said. —I don't.

And then he made a graceful segue for which I am to this day eternally grateful.

—But what about this gravel.

It was true, and it was something to which we could at long last agree. The gravel was there, everywhere, all around us and undeniable. I had in fact been hobbling through it for some time, appropriately shod for nothing so much as a Kasbah and quite inappropriately shod for anything else at all. Particularly for an excruciatingly long stroll through gravel.

I showed him my footwear, flat and lovely and procured for a pittance at a stall in a sandy place we'd once been. He nodded, first admiringly, and then, catching on, with sympathy.

—They'd be lovely for a Kasbah, he said.

—Isn't it true.

—Not quite right for all this, he added, sweeping his fine arm, which I had so recently enjoyed caressing, across the grand graveled landscape.

—Not quite at all. But I noticed something then. —Could we perhaps take one of the golfing carts.

They were littering the gravel and almost all unattended. It was quite an observation on my part, bordering on the epiphanic.

—Don't you think it would be missed, he said.

—There are so many, I said. —If one were missed, another could be easily substituted.

He considered this, and glanced furtively about. The men were going about their busy days, some on foot and some on cart. The carts not in use did not seem about to be in use. If one had sudden use for a cart, there were so many to choose from. It wasn't clear whether the carts were in fact individually Assigned or available indeed for public consumption.

Our hearts beat as one as we boarded a cart.

What I had from past experience and not from naive and ill-considered assumption assumed to be the passenger side of the cart turned out to be the driving side of the cart, so I put my foot to the pedal and drove. It took some getting used to. First I drove the cart very fast and the gravel sprayed up against the bottom like rapid and potentially deadly gunfire. Then I drove the cart a bit slower and that seemed all right.

Pleasant in fact, as though we were on a fine holiday.

Keeping my foot on the pedal and holding the wheel in place

with my knees I pulled a great flowing scarf from one of my secret pockets and tied it around my hair and applied my enormously oversized aviator-style sunglasses to my face.

Now it was much more as though we were on a fine holiday.

We threw our heads back and laughed the carefree laughs of people setting off on a fine holiday.

Tiki Ty brandished a handful of miniature champagne bottles from what must have been a secret oversized pocket of his own, and popped the corks and poured some, bubbling, into small plastic champagne flutes. We clinked plastic glasses and tossed back the champagne in the manner of people celebrating their good fortune at enjoying such a fine holiday.

I wondered if he had tucked within another secret pocket some petits fours and madeleines.

I wondered this out loud, which was accidental but quite to my advantage as he got a devilish gleam in his eye and rooted around about his person. He produced a small wicker basket with a handkerchiefed top and fed me a madeleine with his fingers. Then he fed me a deviled egg, then a spot more champagne, then a delicious chocolated strawberry.

It was a fine time.

It ended too soon.

Tiki Ty pointed and mumbled through a mouth of deviled egg something unintelligible but whose gist I understood because of the pointing. We had come upon a grim whitewashed building with a door and no windows, walled on either side so high that one couldn't see behind it, and labeled with no further explanation and in grim gray paint: BATTERSEA.

# 28

—This is the place then? I said.

Tiki Ty nodded and shoved another deviled egg into his mouth. He had gotten egg everywhere, and the little red speckles that traditionally decorate deviled eggs.

—Sort of grim, I said.

Unintelligible egg mutterings from Tiki Ty.

I mean, there was egg in his *hair.*

—No wonder she runs away, I said.

Unintelligible egg mutterings.

—Do they not allow food inside, I said. —Because, really, you could bring them with you.

Paprika.

Those were the red speckles.

—They allow food, he said, thickly but in at long last an intelligible manner. —They have food too.

—I don't know if I want what they have, I said. I pictured great gray bins of gray foods, slopped onto cheap gray cracked plates by cheap gray cracked ladies.

—I bet you might, he said. He licked admirably far past the perimeter of his lips for stray bits of egg. It wasn't going to correct what he had going on up top, but it helped.

What an exotically long tongue he possessed!

He licked and smacked for a moment more and then we abandoned our golfing cart to its next passengers—perhaps one could only hope the next escapees from this 'Battersea.'

# 29

**There were two robust ladies** behind the front desk, neither one cheap, cracked, nor gray.

Well, one could hardly determine for certain whether they were cheap, but neither lady was cracked, nor gray. Not to the naked eye, anyway. Any cracks, if cracks there were, were kept carefully concealed under starched white layers of linen and expertly applied spackle. Any gray, if gray there was, was expertly dyed away.

—Which one's in need of the rest, one said, not looking up, and then looking up and looking us up and down each in what was meant to be a subtle way, and might have been a subtle way, if one of the ones being looked up and down weren't so impeccably trained in observation and intuition.

—Who isn't, Tiki Ty said jovially.

—True, true, the other lady said.

—There's a little something, the first lady swiped at Tiki Ty's topknot, —in your hair.

Tiki Ty turned to me, pained. —You don't tell me these things? I mean, it's common courtesy.

Both ladies turned to me then, equally pained. —Common courtesy, dear, they echoed. —You don't let a companion go visiting without mentioning a mess of egg up in his hair.

—Where did you get this one, anyhow, one of the ladies asked Tiki Ty.

—Why in tarnation is this one with you, the other said.

—One of Binelli's, he said.

That explained things to their satisfaction, evidently. They evidently knew Binelli and they evidently also knew Tiki Ty, and evidently knew perfectly well that it was neither he nor me in need of the rest, as they'd suggested.

I am not fond of unnecessary chitchat or elaborate subterfuge. I gave a single icy glance all around to express my displeasure.

The two ladies pealed with laughter.

—O dear, you're maybe in need of the rest after all then, one said, as she unhitched a piece of . . . desktop, allowing us to pass from in front of the desk to behind, as it were.

It was really more of a counter than a desk. It was simpler to say desk at first, but I realize now that was misleading.

There were two robust ladies behind the front counter would have been equally simple and infinitely more accurate a statement with which to start this portion of the account. In my defense, it was not intended to be an out and out lie, though that is exactly how it turned out. A bell cannot be unrung, as they say.

Please banish all thoughts of desks, if possible, from further consideration of this description, and let us move then from the extremely compromised point of this scene with all due haste into the next, where every effort will be made, let us all be struck down cold if I lie, to ensure the report's integrity.

# 30

**The next scene** is also terrifically more pleasant to describe.

And when I say let us all be struck down et cetera, that does not constitute my participation in a belief system.

Moving on.

# 31

**I have been to many places** since waking from the silence.

Likely many many more, prior.

I have been in swampland and gravel, sand, ocean, rain forest, and bog. Some places indescribable, having characteristics of neither swampland nor gravel, rain forest nor bog. Nor sand. Nor ocean. And so forth. Some places have been straight clean poured concrete, another entirely encased in liquid. One was so foggy we none of us could see: not each other, not our own hands in front of our faces, not our wretched red incessant tendrils poking out at odd angles just far enough to be caught in our peripheral vision. That last mostly concerned me, and I will say that I rather enjoyed the foggy place. An informal poll taken after the foggy place found the others in agreement; they too enjoyed the respite from my hair.

—And your eyes, especially, The Lamb pointed out.

Which she's had me write in right here though I'd intended to keep stricken these sidewise and for all intents and purposes insignificant comments from the record.

Well there it is. Let it never be said I am not thorough and meticulous with the details, no matter how *sundry*.

All to say, anyhow, if I may be allowed to continue, that I am not naive of place. I'm not from Lungst, or Utah, or Bren, the tenth daughter of the tenth generation of whom only one lone member ever left, and turned up mad three kilometers from the town limits, and was made a quick example of, tied to stocks in the square as a warning to uppity youngsters.

I would not expect a place to surprise me.

But Battersea . . . o Battersea. You surprised me. The grim gray doors opened up upon you, and it seemed color had only just been invented to paint your verdant gardens, your golden walkways, your plum and maize and aquamarine flora. It seemed the sky only came alive above you, reflecting a spectrum of azures so vast and varied one could hardly term them all azure. It seemed the birds of the outside world—yes, even the nightingales of Odille's voice— were to your birds a hack regional orchestra, fine to the untrained ear, yes, but impossible to tolerate once *your* birds were heard. Even your honeybees—yes, you had honeybees—were fatter, lazier, furrier than any honeybee hath ever—

And with *hath* it must cease. With *hath* one knows that one has been waxing poetic, as it were, waxing like a seven-day candle, and there is to be no waxing, poetic or otherwise, in official documents. It is not done.

And yet.

And yet.

It is just as I described it, only more so. Deeper, richer. I hadn't even come to the smells.

# 32

**Naturally, I swooned.**

For some very apparent reasons, all of which have to do with
the grim gray building through whose extremely misleading entrance Battersea can be reached, I had been expecting a horse of
a quite different color. A horse in ragged, stained pajamas, to be
honest. And white and chrome and restraints and rubber.

The two robust and efficient ladies braced me up between them.

—They all do it, one said to the other, over my head.

—True, the other said. —So true.

Tiki Ty was striding ahead, sneaking an egg from his pocket
every few steps. A shaggy dog bounded up to him and tried to
shake him down for an egg but Tiki Ty kicked him away. The dog
was more hurt than an outside dog would have been. This dog,
with its gleaming fur and a shag that would put an outside shaggy
dog to shame, gave Tiki Ty a look more woebegone than ever a dog
had managed, outside Battersea, and walked away with an admirably slow precision, giving Tiki Ty a good long time to think about
what he'd done, and possibly—though the dog wouldn't look back
for anything—reconsider.

Tiki Ty, I knew, would never reconsider. He was immune to the
charms of his own shrimps, but put a deviled egg in front of him—

How many eggs could he possibly have.

The grounds were scattered with small bungalows of all different colors. The one the robust ladies steered me toward had been allowed to remain unpainted, just a rich natural wood that was suddenly the most lovely color I had ever known. The grasses grew wild around it, and the roof was ecstatically thatched, like a child's hair after a long autumn day spent among leaves. Flowers grew up around the door and windows in haphazard combinations. The whole area smelled of honey and lemon and heavy cream and lavender.

I gave my satchel a quick squeeze. Lavendar must have been wondering, after the novelty of a golfing cart ride, and then the strange heavy bodies flanking us on either side, and now the odd set of pleasant smells, and he with no view of any of it and so left to his own imaginings.

If snakes indeed smell.

Can smell.

Not *do* smell. I can answer that myself. Snakes do smell. This one does. Snakes in general, I cannot account for, nor do I care to. But this snake, I have to rub down with liniment at least once a week, and feed special foods that won't rank up his scales, and shake potpourri into his satchel when he's not looking, just to freshen it up a bit.

It enrages him.

It's pretty well worth it.

Lavendar, however, seemed unconcerned with the entire adventure.

One of the ladies knocked at the door.

—You have visitors, she said to the door.

—Two of them, the other said to the door.

—And they have deviled eggs, the first told the door.

—But they're going fast, the other said to the door.

Then they waited.

We all waited, and we waited for what would have seemed an excruciatingly long while anywhere else, but which passed delightfully and without a dull moment, all the wonders of Battersea our only necessary entertainment.

The door spoke suddenly, and urgently.

—Are there still some now.

The ladies glanced at Tiki Ty who again had egg everywhere.

I felt vindicated.

Do you see, I said to them silently, willing them to understand, and think better of me, and perhaps invite me to stay, for some time, at Battersea, what I put up with.

He nodded, groping himself a little.

—There are still some, but very few now, one lady said to the door.

—Could I have one then, the door said.

—We will put one in for you, the lady said to the door.

Tiki Ty handed one deviled egg over with only some reluctance and the lady squatted down, opened the door a crack, and placed the egg just inside. She closed the door gently.

There was movement behind the door. There were chewing sounds. Then a delighted, —Tiki Ty! through a mouthful of egg (had they all been raised in a barn, I couldn't help but think) and the door flung open.

# 33

**Kiki B was not as entirely naked** as she'd been when her acquaintance I'd first made, but nearly so.

She wore now what appeared to be men's underclothes. Baggy beige-ies, if you will.

She did a very excited dance for Tiki Ty and pawed at him some.

She extracted a second deviled egg from the pocket that I do swear was not in any way apparent to the naked eye, and then she stopped her dance and her jubilant fawning and flounced away.

One robust lady entered the doorway and produced the same fuchsia flowered robe from a hook just next to the door. She cleared her throat in a way that was like talking, and it was a language with which the addressee was evidently quite familiar.

Kiki B made a gesture of great pain and dismay, rolling her eyes and clutching at her lanks of still-dirty hair and buckling her knees, but came back to the doorway and stuck out first one arm and then the other and let the lady apply the robe to her form.

Which was, if I'd not mentioned this earlier, somewhat sticky.

But that sounds like I mean something else.

Which is, now that I recall, why I'd left it out in the first place.

Kiki B was to all intents and purposes also sticky to the touch, which is what sticky would seem to indicate. These intents and purposes, however, have no rightful place invading as it were the account and sticky to the touch is not what was meant by sticky at all. What was meant by sticky was sticklike. As in, very much like a stick insect.

O what are those insects that resemble sticks.

—Now you all have a good visit, the ladies said in chorus. They left us to our own company then and bounded out across the grounds of Battersea with surprising buoyancy and grace, considering as I couldn't help but to consider their robustness.

I watched them make their gazelleish way back toward the grim gray building, stopping to splash one another in the fountains and fish pools along the way, and I admit I breathed a really idyllic sigh as I turned back to the room.

Kiki B was in repose atop her splendid bed.

The bedcover was what appeared to be silk of the most faded dusty mushroom shade and was indeed silk as a quick feel between the fingers told me.

The pillows were many and plump to the last, covered with quickly rendered and yet somehow evocative blooms. Browns, rich rubies, dull olive greens, and snippets of parsley evoked a very strange feeling in me of what I might describe as memory, if I had memory.

But how could I possibly.

Unless there was a dusty time, sometime. A time bright but let alone for so long that the slanting sun beat the colors mute and no scouring brush ever chased away the motes, bright in their own way until settling on their final surfaces, where they would never again be borne upon that momentary swirling luster.

—Are you waxing, Kiki B said.

I shook any notion of motes from my eyes. She stared at me through that dirty bright hair.

—Waxing? I said.

—Are you waxing, she said again. Then she glanced up to a corner of the room and said, —Or waning.

—I am neither, I said,

—Neither waxing or waning?

—Nor, I said.

—Then what are you doing, she said, disinterested in my grammar lesson.

—What are you doing, I said.

I am somewhat of a master of deflection. I am famous indeed in certain circles. I have been asked to teach intimate workshops dedicated to its art. For an art it is, don't be misled. Very powerful in the right hands, even more so in the wrong.

—There is nothing wrong with your hands, Kiki B said.

I dropped them from where they'd been rubbing each other, palm to palm, with malicious intent.

—What's wrong with your hands, Tiki Ty said. He'd been inspecting a small pot of bamboo, set atop a painted metal washstand next to the bed.

—There is nothing wrong with her hands, Kiki B said. —Don't ruin the bamboos.

—Bamboo, I said.

—No, there are lots of them, Kiki B said, brightening. She leaned up a bit and touched a leaf fondly. —This one's fresh. It just grew. Unfortunately— She ripped another right off its stalk, lower down, and put it to her lips, —when one grows, another goes.

Then she put the leaf in her mouth and chewed it thoughtfully.

—It's a lovely washstand, she said, and nodded several times, pleased it would seem at her own compliment.

It was a lovely washstand. It looked stolen from another time, perhaps, its cheerful faded yellow paint chipping in spots but a fine green patina beneath. The bamboo grew from a pot of shiny aquamarine. There were scarves hung from one side where a thin metal rod outprodded from the stand, also painted in the lovely yellow.

I was a monster in the jeweled room.

—So you two monsters just monstering about then, Kiki B said, twirling a slice of hair around a finger.

I gave her a quick, sharp glance, but she was already, without an ounce of obvious guile, continuing her vagabond ramble. —Having a picnic, having a drive. Was there champagne.

I had perhaps said it aloud, the monster bit.

—There was, Tiki Ty said, giving me a conspiratorial look. —There was champagne galore, and madeleines.

—I have madeleines, Kiki B said. —There are very probably some madeleines in the basket.

She pointed, now very cross, toward a wicker basket just like the one Tiki Ty had produced in the golfing cart, except this one's handkerchief was a raucous crimson.

—There are very likely all the madeleines one could want right there, she said, her finger now shaking with fury. —If one wanted madeleines.

—We've had our fill, Tiki Ty said brusquely, —but thank you.

I would not so much have minded more madeleines, having never, truth be told, had my fill of madeleines. One could always have another madeleine.

But there was some sort of battle of wills and test of strength occurring between Tiki Ty and Kiki B that I felt uncertain about getting in the middle of.

Praying mantises?

Are those the sticky insects?

The boots Binelli had gifted her with, back at the Tiki Barn, were neatly side by side in a corner, toes facing the wall as if being punished.

Kiki B stretched a bare foot out languorously and spread her toes so they fanned out, not one touching a single other.

Having no use for feet not attached to my own ankles, I looked away.

She waved it around some, then, kicking it across the scope of my periphery.

I did not want to see her feet. From my acquaintance with her hair, I could only guess at the state of parts of her that touched the floor. Though the floor seemed clean enough. I stared at a single spot on the wall, a spot of no consequence.

She inchwormed down toward the foot of the bed, retaining the whole way her overall posture of repose, and waved the splay-toed foot right next to my left cheek. Small sounds of exertion came from her and still she shook it.

I grabbed her ankle with snakelike speed and held her foot motionless at an arm's length away.

—Is there something, I said, —that you wanted.

—They gave me a blister, she said, letting her foot go limp in my viselike grip. —See, on the heel, and also some red around the little toe?

The blister on her heel was impressive. It was approximately the size of the pad on my thumb, and filled tightly with clear fluid. The red around her little toe was to all intents and purposes imaginary, but the blister more than made up for it.

I nodded like a doctor, slowly twisting her foot this way and that for inspecting.

She had painted her toenails recently. Perhaps as some sort of recreational crafts activity. There was little to no toenail on the little toe, but she had painted it nonetheless, where a toenail should go. She had bestowed dignity on the little appendage, and I appreciated the gesture.

—They were far too big, she said, gently taking back her foot. —They were made for a monster.

—They all were, I said. —It's a constant source of infuriation.

—Would you like some snacks, she said, suddenly. —Because where did my manners go. I did, I must admit, eat all of the madeleines, some time ago, but there are other things, good things. Go, get the wicker!

I brought the basket to her bed, which I realized I'd come to consider her own private island. I set the basket down with some hesitation upon the fine silk coverlet.

—Here, Tiki Ty said, and he motioned for me to pick it back up. He pulled a good-sized square of checkered tablecloth from somewhere I'd now been able with focused and unrelenting observation to determine was located in the bottoms portion of his clothing.

While he slept that night I'd shake down his clothes for pockets.

Such ingenious pockets, his. Far better than mine, or any of ours.

And I'd meant to ask while at Battersea about those scripted above-the-pocket stitchings they had.

Why were our things so shoddy and second-rate.

I would take it up with Binelli and it would not be futile, though so many things taken up with Binelli were.

It would only take a tailor of reasonable talent.

We could with ease bring in an Italian.

It would not be so very disruptive.

I set the wicker down on the tablecloth. As Kiki B set the places, I reconsidered.

The Italians are always *very* disruptive. The *most* disruptive, I would even go so far as to say.

A tailor of moderate talent then, not quite Italian but whatever was next best.

Maybe a little bit Italian?

—Did I tell you you might like the food, Tiki Ty said. —Didn't I tell you.

It was quite a spread. It was a feast for both the eyes and the gustatory organs. There were small samplings of foods from almost every region. One could, if one liked, travel the world with one's tongue, in order of geography, during the course of this picnic, or perhaps follow the route taken by one of the legendary explorers. One could, conversely, eat salt until one wanted sweet and eat sweet then until one wanted savory, and eat savory until one's tastes turned to fruits and the pulpy juices, and of course on and on until one's palette was dizzied and in need of a seltzer and a sprig of parsley to right it for the cakes course.

We were all beached together on the bed by the picnic's natural conclusion, covered in crumbs. The cakes course had been vigorous. We'd looked one another in the eyes and made a silent commitment, however, to see the thing through to the end. We sallied forth, forged ahead, through black forest and pecan and varieties of pumpkin as well as of course the families sponge, yellow, and angel.

We made a team the likes of which had been sorely missed on this earth since the time of the ancient Olympiads.

We rested. Kiki B tucked her knees up to her chin. She sang a little.

—I now shall take a little nap. Because my brains are filled with sap. If through my brains you take a train—

She gave a deep sigh. Her eyes closed.

We waited patiently.

—You'll find that you won't need a map.

We stuffed the tablecloth into the wicker and put it back on the floor near the door. We brushed the crumbs quietly around the bed but they mostly all rolled into the indent Kiki B's body created. Kiki B swiped at an imaginary bat or bird and let her hand fall back onto the pillow.

She still wore the jangly aquamarine bracelet but something seemed odd about it. Something about the hanging ball part. Which was filled with not a bead but something else, something squashed.

—Is that a grape, I said. We peered at her wrist.

It was a grape, shoved up between the prongs.

She opened her eyes suddenly to our too-close faces but she didn't startle. —Have you ever, she said, —kept a turtle.

Then she did startle. —Wait, wait, she said, pointing a tired finger toward me. —I have your note.

—You gave it to Binelli, Tiki Ty reminded her.

—I gave Binelli *his* note. Now I have hers.

—But you'd said it was for me, I said. —In the first place.

—But we all knew better didn't we, she said. —Wait, it's somewhere around here.

She felt at her pockets and cast about on the washstand and peered blinkishly around the room. Then she remembered.

—It's in the boot, she said. —I cannot possibly get up. Please will you take it on your way.

That was all from her. I reached my hand deep down into the left boot where there was nothing but damp, and then into the right boot where there was a folded-up piece of paper, just like the one she'd handed to Binelli. Except this one was damp. I held it with the very tips of my fingers toward Tiki Ty and he put it somewhere deep within his garb, o that wondrous garb, whose secrets I would learn in stealth, whose mysteries I would uncover by night.

We took our leave.

# 34

**Occasionally things would occur** to me.

For instance: Washing my face with my fine Binelli-issued cleansing milks, at the familiar Tiki Barn basin, before the familiar cracked Tiki Barn mirror, which tore approximately one quarter of my face quite asunder from the rest, it occurred to me that up in the very outskirts of my hairline, in that one lonely quarter of disembodied forehead, I could spy what appeared to be a thin spray of freckles.

I leaned in very close.

I examined the smatter.

It occurred to me of course also that it might just be dirt. We'd had quite a ride in the golfing cart, with gravel spraying up at certain early intervals, and we'd also spent some amount of time in the bungalow of an indisputably dirty person. We'd feasted. There were any number of methods and means by which a small determined flecked field of dirt might affix itself to my face and settle in.

The specks in question, for instance, were not red, as one would expect freckles to be upon a redheaded person, but rather a dull beige. Like dirt.

They did not however move around like mites or motes.

It was possible that my otherwise careful cleansing did not regularly extend all the way up to my hairline. It was possible that the combination of cracked mirror and my own impatience with the twice-daily Binelli-regulated task had resulted in my regularly missing the spot.

I dipped a finger in the soapy basin and wiped it experimentally across the area in question.

The spots remained in place.

The dirt if it was dirt was perhaps quite built up.

I could be, admittedly, very impatient with the washing-up.

I scraped a fingernail lightly across the spots.

The spots remained.

I used the washcloth just a bit and succeeded in reddening the general area, which made seeing the spots more difficult.

The redness took some time to fade.

In that time, The Lamb began wondering in her worst complaining voice what was taking me so very long at the basin and had I been quite drowned and if so might she roll aside my poor bloated body so she too could take care of her evening's washing-up and I hadn't the time then to do any more close examination of the interesting immigrant population thriving at my face's border.

But it occurred to me that I possibly had the potential to grow freckles.

# 35

—So how was the Kiki B, The Lamb said.

All the washings-up had been done and we were enjoying a fine evening.

Very casual was The Lamb. Very cool. Very quiet. Binelli was in after all the room.

—Was she all disrobed again, Murphy said, less cool. —Was she all—

—Slippery? I said.

Whence the universal male delight with water. I excused myself briefly for a spritz.

Binelli said nothing. He was acting as though he were rolling a bowling ball down a smooth paved lane for strike after strike. He was acting this way in all seriousness: picking up the ball, holding it up to his chin, glaring into the distance at the enemy pins in need of swift and violent eradication.

Except there were no pins. Nor ball. Nor smooth, paved lane.

One had to admire his twin powers of concentration and imagination.

He didn't even glance at my freshly dampened form.

I excused myself briefly to change into a baseball jersey, and spritzed again.

—Are you having night sweats, The Lamb said.

—She was fine, I said. —She was dry. She was partially clothed and she fed us a picnic.

Binelli made the hushed cheer of a large crowd. He raised his fists in incendiary triumph. He glanced over at us.

We gave him a thorough cheer.

—She's not *the* Kiki B, Murphy said then.

—Well is there another, The Lamb said.

It was ascertained that there was not.

—Well then, The Lamb said. —And how was the Puppet Man.

She adjusted her curls, putting them all behind her shoulders and then bringing one black thicket back in front. Then she switched them. —Which way, she said, showing us. She held a massive handful of hair in each hand and brought them forward and back, one then the other, until we reached a consensus.

—The Professor was of interest, I said. I like to hold my cards tight to my chest. What with so much else being out in the open.

Though not, I realized, so much my chest. I pulled at the jersey collar. I held my cards a little farther out and tried to stretch my chest to meet them.

—Are you having a spasm, The Lamb said.

—And how is your Investigation, I said, turning to Murphy. —I haven't even heard.

—It's all up on rooftops, he said, —I'm afraid.

Binelli gasped the incredulous gasp of a thousand rapt fans, then cheered.

We gave him a half-hearted cheer. His bowling matches do go on, and there's very little suspense as to the outcome.

Though we could, I suppose, have at any point groaned sympathetically.

—And you, I said to The Lamb. —Yours is the Next to Worst if I remember correctly.

She smiled a loathsome smile. —If you say so, she said. —If that's what you say. I'm sure you must be correct. What with your super-correct memory and everything.

—Well Binelli had said, I said. I tried to remember without my report being just then handy precisely what he had said. It was some time back, and amidst such confusion. But Murphy was the Most Hated? And The Lamb was quite unpopular as well? And I, while certainly objectionable, was the least objectionable of the group?

—Binelli says a lot of things, The Lamb said mysteriously. Her hand darted to her hair and she paused. —Were you quite sure this way was best.

—There's no question, Murphy said. He jangled his pockets against the tension in the room.

Binelli's fists were raised and he cleared his throat.

Then he said ahem.

We cheered a little bit.

Binelli shook his head in disgust. He fondled his big imaginary ball.

—What is it then, I said. —What's your Assignment.

Although the Puppets hadn't so far and right off the bat turned out to be terrible, I still preferred to be only the Third Worst.

—Let's just say, The Lamb said, —my skills are being put to excellent use.

She could not contain her glee, which I felt bode badly for my place in the hierarchy. Though The Lamb has been known to ribaldly lie. As excellent as I am in the art of deflection is she in the arena of misinformation.

Her Assignment was probably quite crummy. Perhaps not all up on rooftops, but quite crummy all the same.

—Did you answer whether she was barefoot, Murphy said.

—Did you ask. His jangling was making Lavendar antsy. My mood was such that a squeezing would be most unwelcome. Unless the squeezing was of Murphy. Or The Lamb.

—Yes, yes, was she wearing the boots, The Lamb said, waving her hair about happily and lowering her voice further. She became solicitous, tugging at my too-short sleeves. —Did she ruin them? Were they quite ruined?

Binelli scratched a final score on his scorecard and waved it around.

Although he had no scorecard, we clapped with varying degrees of enthusiasm. Binelli naturally was the victor. He brushed off the adulation of the crowd and deigned to fraternize with us.

—What's going on, he said.

—Strategy, Murphy said.

It was always the right answer, and no one wanted to involve Binelli in any talk of the boots. What if they were quite ruined. It could not be anticipated how he might react. I thought of Kiki B asleep and disrobed on her idyllic bed. I worried for her, though I knew the boots were not at all ruined. Not at all. Only a bit damp, which is to be expected, with no socks, and leather.

I hadn't examined them for scuff marks or paint.

I rued my carelessness.

—The Puppets were rather small, I said. Deflection works in myriad ways.

—Small, Binelli said. —Really.

—Quite small in fact.

—Quite small. Are you sure.

—Sure as shooting, Murphy muttered, jangling furiously. He was, I suspected, still wondering after the status of Kiki B's feet. Were they shod? Bare? Were they resplendent with elongated monkey-toes? Were they jeweled, festooned, flashing with bits of silver and fish-scales?

Lavendar slithered from his satchel.

—I am reminded, I said, —of an Incident.

—I don't understand, Binelli said. —Were you looking at the right Puppets?

It was a fair question. I had interrogated, after all, the incorrect Puppet Man at a certain point in the early going. But on the matter of the Puppets themselves, I had little doubt.

—They were the ones he showed me, I said.

—Mr. Uppal.

—*Professor* Uppal, I said. —Yes.

I see. Binelli looked hard at my companions, who looked not at him but likewise hard, elsewhere.

—Could we possibly, if you would all be just ever so kind, have a bit of privacy.

He pronounced it in the British way.

Murphy and The Lamb crept from the room. Murphy did jangle once in daring defiance once he had reached the doorway, and Lavendar slithered after him.

—How small, Binelli said. —Like midgets?

—Much smaller than midgets, I said.

—Like babies?

I paused for dramatic effect and Binelli leaned in scandalously close.

—Like fingers, I said. —Like perfect little fingers. If fingers had faces and grace.

—Could you perhaps, Binelli said, becoming ever so slightly shrill, —please start from the beginning and tell me on a minute-by-minute basis exactly what occurred at the residence of Mr. Uppal?

—Professor, I said. It had seemed a minor point the first twelve times Professor Uppal had corrected me yet here I was practically as shrill as Binelli himself, practically grabbing his shoulders and shaking and shaking as I screamed Professor! Professor! Professor!

I am a consummate professional. I should have liked to but I engaged in no shaking. I kept my hands to my sides and kept my tone steady. I repeated myself only once, with authority.

—Professor.

Binelli was silent and I was silent, and we shared the salient silence for enough time for me to wonder after my overall aspect of dampness. Was it time to respritz. Would a temporary adjournment of the meeting be frowned upon.

It would. Binelli said again ahem and I wondered whether this was something new he was trying on and if so how much longer he would keep it up before abandoning it to the scrap heap of phrases and twitches and affectations to which all such some-suches eventually retire.

A bit longer, evidently. He ahemed me again and I recounted in sparkling detail a minute-by-minute account of my time at the Uppal residence.

Most of it you will recall.

You perhaps lack the observational gifts with which I am inbued, and you likely possess no capacity for precision and retention, in which case you may page back through Sections 17 through 21 and refresh your poor tired memory; the report, however, need hold no such baggage. I did include in my recounting to Binelli the sordid details of Lavendar's escapades with the kitchen and the kitten, at risk of raising his ire but in the interest of professionalism and honesty and because, as The Lamb had so unnecessarily mentioned earlier, Binelli finds out everything eventually anyway. I included, however, quickly upon the heels of this installment of the episode a transcript of a conversation I'd had, on my way down the cobbles, with Odille, after.

She'd walked me out because she was bereft, because the house seemed too quiet, too empty without her sweet but slow, too-slow kitten, and also because she had to go meet Rogan. What she'd said, to be more precise, was, —I'll walk out with you. I have to go meet Rogan at his studio.

Before this, when I'd coaxed the misshapen and sated Lavendar back into his satchel and the Professor had suggested the several days' delay before a second meeting and suggested as well that I visit next time sans serpent and retired to his study to force down whatever remained of the sake, and Dame Uppal had steadied her own hands not with liquor or pills but with a tall glass of orange juice and a pinning away of stray wisps of hair, Odille had run hands through her own hair and wiped her eyes and looked intently into a looking glass hung in the Uppal hallway.

Which is to say, Odille readied herself for her public.

Readied as such, when she referred to a Rogan I inferred using logic that this Rogan was a gentleman friend of Odille's. I'd said, as we strolled across the cobbles, which were a bit of a moot point amidst so much gravel, —Is Rogan then a gentleman friend.

—Rogan's *wonderful,* Odille said, quite forgetting her profound grief. —He usually comes here—Daddy loves him, they disappear into that study and study the Puppets for hours together—he's the only one who cares, you know; Daddy says Rogan's like the son he never had—but he's been working on a big project and can't ruin his concentration so much anymore. He won't let me see it—I know it's wonderful, it's all wonderful, what he does, he's quite a genius—but he does need to eat, you know, and have coffee, and croissants to dip into it, so I pick him up there and we have a diner, close by, you know.

—What genius, I said, a throwaway comment that gave me more time to absorb her torrential outpouring of speech.

It worked. She nodded and glowed in his agreed-upon genius.

Binelli nodded as well.

—I see, he said. —And did you walk with her to the Rogan studio, or to the diner, or partway perhaps to either.

—I walked with her the part of the way that was on my way, I said. —I walked her only that far and then I veered off in my own direction.

—So you know the way she went, he said.

—I do.

—And you could recount for me what way that was, Binelli said.

He was not so terribly angry about the Lavendar incident and I was pleasing him beyond any of our wildest dreams.

—I could, I said, and I did. I congratulated myself on my excellent sense of direction in lieu of outside congratulations, which are never easily forthcoming from Binelli, though he certainly brims on the inside with pride. I patted myself figuratively though not literally on the back, my poor pat-starved back, and my back tingled with pride at a job well done.

Binelli made conversation-adjourning motions.

I wanted to bask. I tried to detain him.

—So I should see, I said, —if I can't uncover some midget-sized Puppets then, next time. It's the midget ones we're after then, yes?

—Well, you'll see. I trust you'll figure it out.

Binelli, I can say with almost complete certainty, though it is of course impossible to prove, then patted me figuratively on the back.

I tingled with all my might.

—Yes, I said.

—Perhaps you'll pick up, Binelli said, —some polishing cloths as well. As long as you're out.

Binelli took his leave.

# 36

**I determined to figure it out** and determined to do so beyond all expectation. I would do it with aplomb and vigor and ruthless callowness, or probably more correctly, callow ruthlessness. I would figure it out and return to Binelli with it all figured out and delicately dampened and my baseball jersey sticking in several devastatingly fetching ways to my skin. And some polishing cloths as well. And there would be no more talk of who was the Third Worst.

# 37

There were, of course, certain blips in the overall graveled landscape.

Or, to not circumnavigate the point to death: We came across during the course of a Binelli-mandated constitutional what appeared to be a golfing exhibition. In that it was not what one sees when one comes across an actual golfing *contest,* with its long green lawns and a minimum of gravel, where the men move about freely though according to some preordained plan. A bit like stage-acting.

O, to participate in some stage-acting.

I mean to say, they move from one station to another, between which lie stretches of grass, only grass!

This was not like that.

It was still all over gravel. However, behind largely ceremonial chain-link barriers, men on small plots of glorious grass went through the usual machinations such golfing men make, with a golfing club and a small white ball perched precariously on a small white stand. Which is to say, they waggled and groaned and scoped myopically into the distance et cetera.

The Lamb unbuttoned the uppermost button of her prancy white button-down shirt.

The men were of an age that could be described as middle-to-upper. Upper-age? Middle-to-late? Middle-to-old. They wore the latest in golfing fashion, which mimics the most out-of-date in golfing fashion almost perfectly, in that golfing fashion does not progress at the breakneck pace of other sorts of fashion, say young ladies' fashion, in which one's coat hardly lasts through a snowstorm before it becomes passé.

The latest in golfing fashion involved plaids, white socks, short pants, and collared shirts. The collared shirts were for the most part in various hues of what one associates generally with springtime.

The Lamb unbuttoned the next button down and then the next, and mopped ungracefully at her brow, which had beaded up ever so slightly with a minor sheen of perspiration.

It was not even remotely hot.

The men, after long-suffering bouts of thought and squattings and peerings toward some unidentified goal, would at long last stand quite still, swing the clubs behind their backs, and unwind like springs in the general direction of the ball. As often as not, this would be a false alarm. They would in fact have swiped at an area just to the left or to the right—depending on their handedness—of the ball, upsetting only a small square of turf, a tuft of sod. This in itself was a fascination to watch. I assumed them then to be quite adept golfers, managing to so deftly *not* hit the blatantly protruding target but only the air a hairsbreadth away from it. If it were, in fact, done on purpose. Which I assume it to have been. Done. On purpose. Given that these strokes were not immediately followed by any display of frustrated histrionics but rather with a moment of thoughtful contemplation, perhaps a minor adjustment as to stance, another gaze toward some invisible hole.

The Lamb released her ample hair from the industrial-sized barrette required to rein it in. She shook it all about. It fell fetchingly down her back in long black ringlets. It grazed teasingly the sides of her face in mischievous tendrils. It brought out the pink of her cheeks, the black of her eyes, the white of her teeth.

It served her well, that hair.

I coveted, I might as well admit, that hair.

Sometimes I did.

The Lamb flicked out her tongue and licked it all along her lips, twice.

Binelli stopped walking. As did we all, he being the official pace-setter.

—What, may I ask, Binelli said in a very carefully controlled tone, —do you think you're doing.

This was directed at The Lamb but I formulated my own answer in case I became unwittingly a subject of this interrogation.

Her high color went higher. Her cheeks brightened further, her eyes gleamed.

—Whatever do you mean?

She had developed an ever-so-slightly-Southern accent.

—What I mean, Binelli told The Lamb, —is this little display you seem to be making for the benefit of these golfing men. Who are portly men. Out-of-shape men. Elderly men.

If I had wanted some attention right then, I would have pointed out several examples of the golfing men who were less of these qualities than the others—less old, for example, or less portly. I was still however working on my previous answer, which although seeming less and less like it might prove necessary, had become a pleasing sort of puzzle for me in the conversational gaps.

The Lamb was causing these conversational gaps by her admittedly quite obvious ogling of said men. Her skin was goose-pimpled along the arms, causing the dark hair there to fur. There were other instances on her person of standing up at attention. Two instances, to be precise.

Front and center.

Binelli noticed these as well. He shook his hands in front of her face as if to wake her from a trance. He stomped his fine boots loudly upon the gravel.

The Lamb blinked up at him.

—Does this, Binelli said, calmer now, —have anything whatsoever to do with *Lolita*?

I forgot the small pleasing mental puzzle with which I was wrangling and focused my attentions more staunchly on the conversation that almost certainly was no longer going to require its triumphant completion.

The Lamb curled a curl around her index finger. She glanced from under her long black lashes sidelong toward the golfing men.

—*Lolita*? I said.

—It does, doesn't it. Binelli nodded thoughtfully.

—*Lolita*? I said.

—I thought this might, Binelli said, —happen. I thought it might happen and I weighed long and hard the potentially disastrous consequences of your taking this Assignment against the benefits of your taking this Assignment and the scales came up ever so slightly on the side of benefits although now, now, it seems unclear—

I cleared my throat more loudly than would be necessary to actually clear my throat and said, —What was this then about *Lolita*?

—but having made the original decision, Binelli said, —with a clear mind and pure heart and knowing this might happen but it would be for the greater good and would only in any case be a temporary condition—

I had never really heard this sort of monologue from Binelli before but fascinating as the scenario was, there were more important issues at hand.

—Binelli. I waved my hands in front of his face and stomped my less-fine-than-his shoes upon the gravel in the same manner of his own display of just a moment ago, and Binelli snapped to.

—Finley.

—Binelli.

—Was there something you required?

—Is The Lamb. Playing. The role. Of. Lolita. On the *stage*, I wondered aloud in carefully measured tones, whose measure I lost the tiniest bit of control over near the end but which for the most part was tightly and commendably reined in.

—If The Lamb proves able to handle the Assignment.

Binelli was less answering my question than offering The Lamb a vague but pointed threat.

The Lamb seemed to have not heard him. There were so many of the men, all about.

—Did it occur to anyone, I said, this *anyone* directed with the most scathing and dripping sarcasm toward Binelli himself, —that perhaps Someone Else might be the more appropriate Agent for this stage-acting Assignment?

—It occurred to Someone, Binelli said, —that Someone Else might become so immersed in that Someone's play-acting that Someone might in fact lose sight quite dangerously of the Matter At Hand. It occurred to Someone that Someone Else's failure to maintain even the slightest toehold on reality might jeopardize not only the Assignment itself and the well-being of those involved but also the health of the entire Enterprise. It occurred to Someone as a far-fetched notion—

It was no longer clear whether Binelli was explaining to me why I had not drawn the Assignment or berating The Lamb for her general behavior but I thought it wise to interject what I supposed to be perhaps the most key factor at hand. Preceded wisely on second thought by the perhaps second-most key factor at hand, something off-speed, to weaken Binelli for the first.

—You know how I've longed to do some stage-acting.

Then I hit him with my fastball.

—And I am, after all, Russian.

The blows brushed him back. He finally turned to me, Binelli did, and shook off his cobwebs. And his mouth began to open, and as what was about to come out were the words I'd been longing to hear, for what suddenly seemed like all the time I'd been alive that I could remember, which admittedly was not so very long, but long enough in the mysterious way of time, I closed my eyes to hear the words, o the words, which would say some things along the lines of yes, Finley, and born to play Lolita.

Instead, what I heard, there in my waiting posture—my most pleasing posture, I was thinking, as I waited for the words that would sound so sweetly in my ears—my most pleasing ears, I realized, shapely if somewhat on the smaller side—and basking in the anticipated glow of . . . anticipation . . . was the voice of The Lamb.

—Lolita wasn't Russian.

Everything stopped. The golfing men perhaps didn't stop though they moved so slowly it would be hard to tell stopping from continuing doggedly along in their desperate quest. But everything else by which I mean to say Binelli and myself and the ubiquitous crunch of gravel underfoot stopped.

—Pardon me.

—Lolita wasn't Russian.

I again begged most sincerely her pardon.

—Mr. Vladimir Nabokov, the writer of the story that is titled *Lolita*, was in fact a Russian man. But he didn't write the story in Russian, though he wrote some other, lesser to my albeit humble opinion, things in Russian, and the character in question, Lolita, was not in fact a Russian girl.

I wrung my hands slightly while I tried to regroup.

Hand-wringing is more difficult than the stories make it out to be. It feels quite unnatural. Even drecked in the bottomless depths of pure and abject despair, one has a *sense* of oneself doing the wringing, which creates a self-consciousness in the wringer and presumably a twinge of suspicion in the wringees.

In this case, Binelli and The Lamb.

—What the hell are you doing with your hands, Binelli wondered.

—Are you trying to wring your hands, The Lamb said almost simultaneously.

They caught each others' eyes then and laughed a little bit, forgetting for the moment their mutual wrath. They then it would appear came to the again-simultaneous decision to capitalize on their renewed goodwill by furthering the joke.

—And you thought you might like to do some stage-acting, The Lamb said.

—Can you imagine? Binelli said.

They stage-acted me stage-acting then, rolling their eyes like terrible monsters at one another and gesticulating wildly. Binelli actually fell to his knees, clutching at his heart. They groaned and writhed and most of all wrung their hands dramatically.

—And I suppose, I said with dignity, —you could do so much better.

The Lamb rose to her full posture then, and looked me directly in the eyes, and wrung her hands. I almost clutched her to me, so deep was the pain she conveyed with those hands.

Even Binelli was silenced. We watched The Lamb and her tortured hands until she just as easily as she had begun halted the wringing and shook them out, as though they were limber athletes who had concluded a good day's physical training and were now getting into their comfortable sleeping clothes to crank up the pianola and eat home-baked cookies.

—Anyway, Binelli said to The Lamb, me and my claims to her Assignment evidently laid to rest, buried, and ivied over until the carefully etched words were barely discernible, —could you try not to let your Assignments get the better of you? Could you try to maintain some sort of professional sense of separation? I ask this not to stifle your talents or curb your enthusiasms, but simply to save you from exhaustion and burnout. As such a valued member of this Enterprise. And so forth.

—I'll try, The Lamb said. She glanced with only the slightest watering-about-the-mouth toward the golfing men once more, and then beamed up her aggravatingly-high-watted smile toward Binelli.

—I'll try.

# 38

**As a Russian,** however reluctant, I took a substantial Slavic pride in not only my mastery of the Russian tongue—which I speak to this day with impeccable accent—but in my vast knowledge of the Motherland's accomplishments and persons-of-note in the fields of art and culture and government and weapoury.

The Lamb's triumphant trouncing of me then in Nabokov-knowledge really chapped my hide.

It would behoove me to resume my studies, I considered. It would behoove me to really bone up on my Bodrov and Bunin, Brodsky and Borises of every stripe; but dips into the Tiki Barn's stable of literary offerings inevitably disappointed.

I read California crime novels instead into the night and lamented at length The Lamb's freakish intelligence, a matter on which I have perhaps previously indicated I hold a few theories.

**39**

## Theory No. 2 Regarding The Lamb's Freakish Intelligence

The Lamb had the mis- or good fortune—that determination to be made ultimately by the impartial observer, when all facts are at hand, and some distance into the future—to be born of a large-ish commune, bunkered up in the hills of an undisclosed region. The names and characters of her specific parents were not important, nor had those specific parents any actual inkling that they were the specific parents, having given the child as was customary over to the care of the child-care area upon her birth. Children, like food and garb and trinkets and mates and feather-beds, belonged to no one and everyone in the commune all at once. Children were group property, group responsibility, as were the farm animals and the bedraggled crops and the unruly but robust rows of tobacco and the ambitious solar dome, whose long-term feasibility was the cause of some question but whose care, maintenance, and anticipated rewards were and would be shared and shared alike.

The children's lives were carefree and unregulated. The adults of the commune wished above all else to create and sustain a generation and subsequent race of humanity unburdened by the burdens society had so callously inflicted on themselves. Burdens of guilt, yes, and familial hang-ups, burdens of 'sex' and 'shame' and 'gender' and personal 'identity.' They wished their collective children's imaginations unquashed by an intolerant bureaucratic regime, which valued competition and mathematics so highly. They did not want any child to feel ever inferior, or ever smug, ever righteous or trumped or ugly. They offered the children no standardized testing, no contests involving feats of strength, no choosing of teams, no mirrors. The children were instead encouraged to choose for themselves, at their own volition, the instruments through which they might best Express Themselves. They would be buoyant souls, vibrating vessels of creativity, liberated from the daily fears and lists of self-searching questions and reprimands, which would only hold them, as they the adults had been held, back from their full potentials.

The children were encouraged to name themselves. They were encouraged to do this at a very early stage in their development, with limited vocabularies and, truth be told, limited fields of vision and landscape from which to choose their special words.

Many children chose Lamb. Many children chose Tree and Sky. More children than it had been hoped chose Goat. The rotating bands of child-care-givers had to toss their negativity toward Goats from their heads, shaking it from their hair like leaves, or lice. Like lice, these negative thoughts were tricky to disentangle. The caregivers, not raised themselves within a carefree and unregulated paradise, accidentally and with remorse thought just a touch less of the Goats, and a little bit more of the Skys, and almost worshipfully of the Rains.

A child who proclaimed itself Rain was—always in secret and by many different adults—given treats.

The adults still had some hang-ups.

The commune's strong views on hierarchies and labeling and mathematics and damage to small forming brains being what they were, the educational arena was, much like the solar dome, an easier question to deal with in theory, over cocktails, and was very much still being worked out when The Lamb passed through.

The educational arena was, in fact, quite lacking.

The educational arena, in fact, differed little from the rest of the children's arenas, as it was not to by any means be limited to any walled-in space—the world was their educational arena!—nor any stock areas of study—the children would know what to study; they need only look around!—and so the children were often not aware of what they were supposed to be doing.

To banish *supposed-to-be* from the vocabulary had been an early tenet of the commune.

Nor were the child-care-giver adults necessarily specialists in any specific topics.

Even those who were weren't particularly effective in imparting much of use, as those specialist labels were just another of the societal burdens from which they were trying to get out from under.

So the children listlessly stood about, mostly, sometimes chasing one another, sometimes vaguely doodling with sticks, sometimes pulling the wool from sheep, which elicited great protests from the sheep and therefore great amusement from the children.

Sometimes they would organize large-scale games, with rules they'd created themselves, but whenever sides were to be drawn up, the adults would step in and offer alternatives. These alternatives were always so stupid that the game would be abandoned and the children would resume their listless private moping.

The Lamb, during the course of one particularly listless summer, had taken to breaking into the residences dotting the property. Not that breaking in was necessary; the doors had no locks, and all inside each was for public consumption. But she took to stepping inside these residences, once her careful observations from the shrubbery indicated the place was alone, and poking about among the things. There was never any use taking anything—it was all hers, as much as anyone's—but she liked to see what was available, anyhow, and to touch these things and put some sometimes in her pockets for redistribution. She liked to recline on the shabby furnishings and snack on the stores of food and—eventually, after much chagrined staring and deciphering, and then

126

many mind-numbing hours of solicited bedtime reading from various adults, whose unfortunate bodies she would have to nestle up against in order to watch the words and learn to associate the symbols with the spoken sounds but with otherwise no help at any point from any adult whatsoever, who had collectively forgotten that children rarely if ever sprang literate from the womb—read their books and, in one dwelling whose primary occupant apparently had not been able to relinquish this single outside influence: general-interest magazines.

It was on one such day, late in the summer, when The Lamb was interrupted midway through an article about the kidnapping of Ash Berlin, a moniker belonging to whom The Lamb did not know but which she found magnificently enviable. As she read of the heist and its tear-stained aftermath, she wished that she too, as the Ash of the article surely must have, come across a distracted smoker as a toddler and pointed to the gray-hot tip and proclaimed herself proudly its equal.

She was interrupted in this and surrounding thoughts by a knock at the door.

It was not a custom with which The Lamb was familiar. She froze but had not the background to consider it a summons to rise from her repose and move toward the door and open it with a pleasant and welcoming expression. People traditionally in her experience simply moved in and out of enclosures, doors just another permeable membrane—like skin, as some of the children had recently discovered.

The knocking was more firm then, and accompanied by voices.

—Is someone home, the voices said.

The Lamb thrilled just a bit, though she couldn't have said why. She was *allowed*.

And yet, a tiny shiver.

The doorknob twisted very gently and two men in identical clothing darkened the doorway. They peered inside, making note of The Lamb on the couch but seeming to expect something more.

The Lamb watched quietly.

—Are you alone here then, the men said.

She could not distinguish one from the other.

—Are your parents home, the men said.

—No. Of that The Lamb could be sure. Whichever of the hugely hairy adults were her parents—and she had, as did each of the other children, her suspicions as to which were whose—they were certainly not here. Nor home, in any sense of the word.

The men looked at one another. —Could we come in then, they said. —We won't take up much of your time.

She nodded, sitting up straighter. She was perhaps being kidnapped and she didn't want to miss any of it slouching lazily on the pillows.

—What's your name, the men said.

—Ash, The Lamb said. She hadn't even thought about it beforehand; it just slipped out.

It felt good. —Ash, she said again.

—Well Miss Ash, the men said, losing some of their formality and becoming as solicitous as they could manage, their training being what it was, —we have a special offer for you and aren't you the lucky girl to have been home on such a fine summer's day to hear it.

She was beyond lucky, The Lamb knew. Nothing of any import had happened since the day of her birth, and no one had ever been selected for a Special Offer except for Rain and Rain and Rain and Rain and Rain, who sometimes found extra cookies in their pockets for no good reason that anyone could notice.

—I see you like to read, the men said, indicating her somewhat crumpled magazine.

—A child who loves to read, the men said, —now there's a welcome sight.

—A child indoors on a fine summer's day, enjoying her reading, now that's a right welcome sight, the men said. —And a happy co-incidence besides.

—Do you ever find yourself left with questions after reading, the men said.

—Do you ever want to look further into a topic raised by one of your general-interest magazines, the men said.

—I read books too, The Lamb said. She indicated some piles of bossy hardcovers, which mostly said the same things the adults always did.

—I can see you're a bright one, the men said, beaming. —What a lucky coincidence we knocked on your door today.

The men nodded at one another and then lay their briefcases upon the table. They knelt awkwardly on the lousy pillows that served as seating in this particular residence, bringing themselves to her eye level. They snapped the briefcases open with an official series of clicks and then turned the briefcases around so their open mouths faced The Lamb.

Each briefcase contained a book, but not a book like was found in the heap on the floor, or in any of the heaps on any of the floors of any of the residences on the whole of the property.

For one, these books were new.

For another, they were blue, and embossed with shiny gold lettering on the front.

One man's briefcase book was embosssed with a large golden A. One man's briefcase book was embossed with a large golden B. The Lamb traced the first of these great golden letters.

—You like that one, right, the men said.

—It's the first letter of your name, the men said. —What a wonderful coincidence, isn't it.

—Do you know what these books are, the men said.

The Lamb shook her head.

—These, the men said, —are encyclopedias. In these books, beginning with this A volume, you can find all the answers to all your questions about everything in the world.

—And we, the men said, —would be happy to leave this A volume with you, right here, right now, if you think you might get some use out of it.

—Would you, the men said, —do you think, get some use out of it?

The Lamb nodded. She could hardly wrest her eyes from the letter. She was not, she understood, being kidnapped, and yes, she was a bit disappointed. But then, this book. She wanted it more than she'd ever wanted anything. She wanted it to be all hers, and not collective. She would agree to any terms.

—We'll come back in, let's say, one month's time, the men said. —We'll bring the B volume.

—Every month, the men said, —we'll bring you a brand new letter. In twenty-six months, you'll have learned more than maybe any other little girl in all the land. You'll be so chock-full of knowledge about everything from ants to . . .

—Zephyrs, the men said, —that you won't even know what to do with yourself. They'll all be saying, though, what a bright little girl, to know so much, about so many things.

—They'll all be talking about it, the men said.

But they would not as it turned out all be talking about it, not at the commune. Because The Lamb guarded the books with her life. She pored over each volume, each page, each and every month for twenty-six months. She found Volume S particularly illuminating. She read greedily, in fear that the men would return to make their monthly exchange before she had finished. And the commune turned out to be the perfect place to conduct so exhaustive an endeavor, because as per the child-care tenets, no one questioned The Lamb's whereabouts. No one wondered whether it was healthy for a child to take so much Alone Time. It was assumed that The Lamb had simply found an interest, a project, a latent genius for something—anything—and that the genius was best administered to, after all, by the being in which it dwelled.

There had been a minor incident, early on, involving the sudden intrusion of the word *Anarchy* into the circle of children, but The Lamb quickly learned that learning was best kept close to one's chest.

It was a tiny bit disappointing for the Fibs. Not to be confused with members of any particular nation's organized sect of Investigators.

For as it happened, the two men were Investigators, yes, for a governmental agency. The nickname Fibs had gained an amused popularity and then taken firm hold well beyond the reaches of the originating body; indeed, the nickname went almost international, save for the quite northernmost reaches, who had their own stubborn slang. The standard suiting, even, had been Officially adorned with a heat-pressed F, peeking from the breast pocket. You could tell the oldest-timers this way, at functions and funerals, slightly out-of-sorts and unamused in their straining hurriedly home-stitched imitations.

As has been previously indicated, the commune was located in an undisclosed region.

The Fibs' mild disappointment arose from The Lamb's sheer voraciousness. Getting the books, complete with tiny recording devices both visual and auditory, into the commune had been a feat. The books, however, had been meant to circulate. They'd been meant to be taken care of carelessly, left here and there, picked up by others, paged through while making meals and sipping wine and perched upon different coffee tables in different dwellings, eavesdropping on the mundane, yes, but also on the secrets, the scandals, the whispered admissions of deep and egregious and rampant wrongdoing.

In The Lamb's care however the cameras, deftly inserted in each volume's stiff leather spine, captured hours on end of tables' topsides and the surprisingly tidy inside of a satchel. The voice recorders caught a lot of labored breathing, fingertips scraping paper.

There were moments, however. The Lamb sometimes, after all, had to be among people, but had grown so quiet and indistinct that the people, when she was around, often failed to even notice her presence. They spoke things they might not—tenets of childcare-giving notwithstanding—have spoken in front of a young onlooker.

The spent tapes each month were some poor intern's painful task to transcribe, but the small bits they yielded were enough. On the day of the sting, a very small special task force snatched up The Lamb, a snatching unnoticed in the general melee.

An unanticipated by-product of the mission's methods: The Fibs had unwittingly—though afterward would never reveal the accidental nature of the coup, accepting all credit for foresight and derring-do, sly as the lie their nickname evoked—created the perfect spy.

# 40

**Dame Uppal herself** greeted me at the door on my next trip to the Uppal estate. She offered a bright smile after subtly glancing about my person for satchels filled with serpents or otherwise equivalently disorderly items I might be intending to introduce into the household. Finding none, she, as I said, offered a bright smile and invited me in.

She was the Dame Uppal of the Study, right from the get-go: hair neatly bunned, clothing kempt, finely drawn kohl about the eyes. The picture of propriety. Not a shred of her sloppy sitting-room doppelganger lingered, lintlike, to indicate that she'd ever existed at all, even when we sat in that sitting room to wait for her perpetually late husband.

Dame Uppal offered me tea, which I accepted gratefully. Leaving Lavendar at the Tiki Barn always caused me some consternation, which only well-steeped chamomile leaves could set to rights. As we waited for the man to bring our tea, Dame Uppal confided that the Professor had in fact gone out that morning, with Odille, on some sort of secret errand, but that he'd been well aware when he left of the time of our appointment and was sure to be back presently. She confided further that soon would be her, Dame Uppal's, fiftieth birthday, and she suspected that the errand concerned this occasion.

Dame Uppal was quite girlish for a handsome woman of fifty.

She confided then that there had been some peculiarity afoot in the household of late, but that it had recently occurred to her that the cause of the confusion, of the seeming lapses in her husband's attentions, could be attributed to festive birthday surprises. She confessed that she enjoyed nothing so much as a fête, and that it was she who traditionally prepared the fêtes, and that the Professor was sure to be finding the task a touch overwhelming, although of course he had many of his own talents which were at least as—if not perhaps more—important than those in the arena of party planning.

She was not in fact as handsome as I'd first judged. There was something lovely in her face, something softer than had initially been conveyed, and though her dressing gown of days of yore had been truly magnificent, the Dame Uppal of this second visit would have blown the old Dame Uppal away in, for instance, a beauty pageant for Women of a Certain Age.

Day of yore, singular, would perhaps be more accurate a sentence fragment.

I congratulated Dame Uppal on her upcoming birthday and then our tea was brought and the Professor followed quickly on the heels of the manservant into the room.

—I've kept you waiting, he said. —Finley, he said.

Was it my imagination in finding him brusque.

Though I recalled that my last visit had not ended well for him and his household, and perhaps he carried some coolness toward me. Could I fault him for his brusqueness.

I could fault him mildly. I was, after all, still a guest.

Dame Uppal had, after all, gotten past it.

I nodded brusquely at the Professor. —Professor, I said.

—I hadn't seen you come in, Dame Uppal said to her husband. —You sneaky thing. Where's Odille? Has she come with you?

The Professor shook his head as if pecked by tiny birds. —So many questions, he said. —I have business pending.

Dame Uppal looked temporarily chastened, but then winked at me. —You see, she whispered.

—The fête is getting to him.

—What are you saying, Professor Uppal said, and then turned to me. —You may bring your tea, he said, and moved imperiously from the sitting room toward the study.

I took my tea and took my leave of Dame Uppal, who looked about the room as if imagining the magnificent celebration that would soon take place there.

I hoped, although I suspected otherwise, that she was correct.

# 41

**The Professor was already** at his Puppets, curtain drawn, by the time I arrived in the study. He was not a terribly tall man, but his stride was long and he carried an air of impatience about him today.

I took my place beside him before the stage. I waited for the glorious bursting into life I had witnessed on my first visit.

I had been, I admit, thinking since then quite a bit and with perhaps more than a professional interest about the Puppets. I had been even eager to revisit the little stage, the little town, the tiny trampled flower beds and the tiny twisted handkerchiefs that were still quite the fashion among the town's dapper gentlemen. I would never have divulged it to Binelli, for fear of being unceremoniously recalled from the Assignment, but I had quite enjoyed these Puppets and the miniature minutiae of their daily lives, watched over with benevolence by the chuckling godlike Puppet Man and his metallic gloves.

The Professor, however, had one glove only halfway wrested onto his hand—he was having some trouble, it appeared, with his fingers—when he yanked it back off and dropped the curtain, casting the eager town into ever longer night.

—It's just all, he said, —so infernally small.

—But that's what's so nice about them, I said, vaguely aware of the irony of my uncharacteristic and impassioned defense of Puppets.

Of Puppets! toward whom I had expressed such scorn and loathing. Of Puppets! to whom I had compared and not, mind you, positively with my Most-Hated Russians. Of Puppets! which I had proclaimed not so very long ago my Most Hated Thing, or at least my Third Most Hated Thing, after only my countrymen and some blue girl whom I'd actually not even remembered of late to hate.

I dedicated a brief fit of hatred toward the too-tall girl in blue but it felt hollow.

I took the girl in blue off my list. I would have to redraw it altogether. I would do it that very evening.

I would possibly take Puppets off the list as well, as long as the Professor didn't get up to anything.

—But think of the possibilities, he was saying.

—If they were for instance midget-sized, I said darkly. I remembered my conversation with Binelli and remembered as I did my Assignment. I was not here to become besotted, no. I was not here to champion any personal preference as to size, shape, or otherwise overall bearing of the objects in question. I was here to carry out an Assignment and I was prepared anew to do so with all appropriate aplomb, vigor, and et cetera.

—Midget-sized, the Professor said. —Yes. But then if midget-sized, well, why not—

—You don't mean, I said.

—Bigger, the Professor said.

—Bigger, I said at the same time.

We stroked our chins and stared at the drawn red curtain, hiding its tiny obsolete town.

I had no beard to stroke, mind you—I am disagreeable to the eyes, yes, but not in that particular way—but I felt I understood at long last why people did enjoy their own so.

The Professor had a bit of a beard.

He perhaps enjoyed the stroking a mite more than I.

Yet it was he who stopped first. Very suddenly stopped, and

very abruptly made for the hidden door in the bookshelves, and very abruptly and even rudely I would say said, —Excuse me then for a moment, will you please.

He barreled into the shelves and upset an entire row of books.

It was very much the wrong set of shelves.

He looked quickly over his shoulder to see if I'd witnessed this embarrassment and adjusted his aim slightly leftward. This time he successfully touched off the mechanism, and the Professor took his leave.

# 42

**His leave was not long.**

I had only enough time to make my way over to the red curtain and pull just a corner askew, revealing the smallest coveted glimpse of those Puppets.

I would definitely take them off my list.

I would perhaps put The Lamb in their place.

It was not a terribly time-consuming string of thoughts but perhaps I had a small unremembered reverie, for the Professor burst back into the study then, through not the bookshelf door whence he had taken his leave, but through the regular study door, leading out to the hall.

—I am terribly sorry, he said. —I am woefully pained to have wasted your time.

—It was no time at all, I said.

I would almost definitely put The Lamb on my list.

—Let us get then right to it, the Professor said, rubbing his hands in the manner of evil chemists the world over. —But pardon me where are my manners, have you had refreshment.

My tea sat where I'd set it earlier, that is to say upon the chess set, where someone, it was plain to see, was in eminent danger of ambush.

Had he not *told* me to bring my tea.

He was quite distracted with the fête.

I gestured toward my cup and he nodded. —Wonderful, wonderful, I could use a spot myself. Odille is just setting down her things, she'll be along in a moment, in the meantime, shall we?

He gleefully tore open the curtain. He gleefully put on his gloves. He gleefully bestowed the tiny town with glorious bursting life. He gleefully looked upon my face, expecting presumably a mirror of gleeful wonder.

I looked straight at the Puppet Man.

I said, —Are they not then infernally small.

His face dropped. All glee drained. The entire town grew heavy with his disappointment. Tiny tangling bodies fell apart, suddenly disinterested in pursuing whatever passion had tangled them together in the first place. A mailman let the mail fall lacklusterly to the ground.

—I thought, the Professor said. —Had I been quite wrong in thinking, the Professor said.

Then he pulled the gloves from his hands, finger by finger, and said, —That's just what Rogan says.

He left the stage uncurtained and sank heavily into his chair.

—Rogan, like the son I never, mind you, had; Rogan, who was the only one—had *been* the only—well, you understand then, Rogan told me, the Professor said, —just of late, mind you, that they weren't after all so terribly amusing, so small you know. But I really thought.

Every shred of professionalism in me dissipated. I went to the Professor and knelt at his knee. I grasped his forearms in both my hands and said, —No, no they're perfect. Just as they are.

And then I went on, I am loathe to admit. The entire foolish transcript shall not sully this report. I went on and on about what hatred I'd always felt for Puppets. About how prominently they'd figured on my list of Most Hated Things. How, until I'd encountered the very small Puppets here before us, and on and et cetera.

I did not put forth my best foot. It was certainly not my most shining moment. I was letting the Assignment get my better and even with this awareness, awareness of both the fact and the certain dreadful string of consequences such foolhardy letting would certainly bring about, I was powerless to stop it.

Instead, I made the Professor put back on his gloves and transform himself into the jubilant Puppet Man once again, and make, to my eternal shame, the lively tiny town live once more just for me.

# 43

**Tiki Ty made us** all the shrimps we liked, as long as we kept him supplied with ingredients. These he would list, in elaborate code, on a long piece of parchment that we were to guard with our very lives until it was handed over to the proprietor of Siam, a specialty store a long walk away. The proprietor would take the parchment from us, be busy for sometimes hours—in the back, in the basement, in the attic, and on the telephone—and then bring us a number of rucksacks filled with the makings. We would never know what was on the list or what was inside the ornately wrapped bundles tucked within the rucksacks, because Tiki Ty held his recipe for shrimps closely guarded.

He understood that his shrimps enticed customers to the Tiki Barn. He understood that people's taste for vintage surfing memorabilia, much like the elusive surf itself, waxes and wanes, but that their taste for exceptional shrimps is uncomplicated and eternal. He understood that if people could replicate his shrimps in their own homes, they might not make so many of the shrimp-intoxicated purchases they later regret, but which regret they forget, next time a hankering for Tiki Ty's shrimps overtakes their good sense.

We, on the other hand, had neither to browse amongst vintage surfing memorabilia nor even get so very far out of bed for our shrimps, as long as we remained willing to make the necessary treks to Siam.

It was an arrangement we all could live with. It was mine and Murphy's turn, which it always was.

The Lamb said she would accompany us part of the way.

I told her that it was not at all necessary. I told her the way was long and ripe with banditos. I told her she might wind up late, traveling with us, as we were easily distracted and Murphy often spilled his marbles, which then took long, tedious times to find in the gravel. I told her sometimes Lavendar escaped in these times, these long, tedious, back-breaking times, scrabbling through the gravel for bright bits of glass, and that once Lavendar escaped, it could be quite some time more before he returned from whatever adventure he was enjoying, and that during this quite some time we had to remain still and in place and available for Lavendar to find.

—You could keep better track of your snake, for one, The Lamb said.

I keep fine track, I said.

—Better track than Murphy of his marbles, I said.

—Which often spill, I said, —and take long, tedious times to find.

—It is, she said, —no matter. If I didn't get to rehearsal until springtime next, they would be there, waiting, with bated breaths and fluttering hearts, for I am their star and there is nothing to be done without me.

Why did she have to rub it in.

We set sail for Siam.

**The way was indeed long** but not, as I'd indicated, ripe with banditos. Banditos hate graveled landscapes. They hate graveled landscapes with as much verve and conviction as they love to separate unwitting travelers from their possessions. Which is much verve and conviction, as you are very well aware, if you have ever been run across by banditos whilst traveling.

Free of banditos, the travel was festive and light, The Lamb's unwelcome presence notwithstanding. We donned jaunty felt fedoras for the journey, making really a day of it, and ate ecstatically of an allotment of shrimps. There had really been packed only enough for me and Murphy, but the introduction to our heads of such fine fedoras made us jovial and generous, so we shared with only a touch of grudging our shrimps and there were plenty, plenty of shrimps for us all!

I told them in more detail about Odille.

—She has eyes of the sky, I said, —which glitter like stars. Her figure is hourglassed. Her voice, I said, —is like the song of a thousand nightingales.

—However, I said, —her miniature is even more fine. Her miniature makes her larger version seem quite obscene.

—So she's obese, The Lamb said, pleased. —Quite obese, which overshadows all her aforementioned clichéd attributes.

—Not obese, I said.

—It's a shame, The Lamb continued. —Obesity. When she might have been quite nice in fact otherwise.

—Obscene, I said. —Obscene.

—A shame, yes, The Lamb said. —But what can you do. Poor fat Odille, poor night-sky eyes, having barely a chance to shine, hidden within those fatty eye-folds.

The Lamb performed the Dance of the Obese, a waddling sort of choreographical sculpture that took for its clay grace and lightness and natural ease of movement, swaddled it in layers of flesh, and gave it a sort of pained dignity that made one feel slightly superior and condescendingly benevolent.

—Poor thing, I said. —Poor obese Odille.

—At least she has her voice, The Lamb said, with unusual generosity. —She could do something with that, perhaps.

—Join a chorus, I said.

—A chorus would be perfect, The Lamb said. —Those flowing robes. One might overlook the unfortunate form.

—The ungainly flesh, I agreed.

—The flatulent grandeur, The Lamb agreed.

The Lamb and I found ourselves in a rare and perfect agreement. We each took a shrimp from the sack and toasted one another with a brisk clink of shell. We sucked the shrimps back in unison and shouted Opa!

—What in the name of all that is good and reasonable is this, Murphy said.

I thought he was wondering after my and The Lamb's agreeing, and toasting, and celebratory shouting of Opa! but he wasn't even looking at us.

He was looking at the angry swollen crowd in front of the theater where The Lamb's rehearsal was waiting only for her arrival to go ahead and take place.

What a crowd it was.

It was a crowd waving banners and signs on sticks high into the air. It was a crowd of deafening volume, with competing chants and hysterical war cries shrilling above their general hubbub. It was a crowd roasting lambs on makeshift spits, and kebobs over fire-pit flames, keeping themselves sustained and festive for what could possibly go on all day, into the night, into an endless series of days and nights fanned by fury and indignation. And lambs and kebobs.

It was a crowd, we suddenly realized, of born-agains, having one of their fabled mild fêtes.

Though it didn't seem so mild, in person.

Why had there been this implication in all the fables of mildness.

Had we misunderstood the unusual vocabulary in the texts.

As we wondered these and perhaps other things, the crowd seemed to, as one great mind, sense our presence on their periphery. The chants died suddenly but for one lone voice that hadn't yet realized the chanting had come to an unexpected conclusion and fervently proclaimed one more time its dedication to the cause before cracking midproclamation and fading in embarrassment.

The spit unashamedly continued its hiss and fizzle through the hush.

Lavendar stirred uneasily in his satchel and I understood that the presence of a snake on our collective person might only serve to strengthen the crowd's conviction of our guilt. I kept tight rein on the drawstring.

O for the impossible arrival of some banditos!

Murphy's pockets jangled furiously.

The crowd moved as one body a little bit toward us.

The crowd's many heads swerved this way and that, consulting with its other heads in a low murmur.

The crowd advanced a little closer, as per its arrival at some conclusion.

—Is there any, Murphy said, —possibility that there is someone else behind us that the crowd wants to shout things at and advance upon.

The Lamb gamely swiveled her head very slowly and slightly to check behind us and answered in the negative.

—I thought not, Murphy said, —but it was worth a glance.

We agreed—again!—that it had been worth a glance, even though the possibility had indeed been unlikely and far-reaching in its optimism.

We commended Murphy in whispers on his ability to retain optimism in the face of such violent opposition.

For it would, we knew, be violent.

It seemed hardly fair, when I considered, that I should be made to pay so violently for The Lamb's coveted Assignment. Hardly fair in the least.

With inspired subtlety I pushed The Lamb forward a bit, looking the crowd in its collective glittering eye and trying to indicate without words that this was the one they wanted.

—Stop jostling me, The Lamb said through gritted teeth. —You horrid *Finley*.

Lavendar's head poked against my fingers, tightly clenched around the top of his satchel. His questioning tongue flicked my skin, testing it for tension.

It would only, I knew, be a matter of time.

I told Lavendar beneath my breath that if he were good and remained in his satchel I would buy him an extra-large quail's egg at Siam.

There is nothing Lavendar loves so well as an extra-large quail's egg from Siam.

We could feel the crowd's hot foul breath on us.

Then we noticed something. Murphy noticed it first. I caught him sniffing. I thought it odd that he was sniffing rather than plugging his nose-holes against the hot foul breath, as were The Lamb and I. I thought it odd, and thought Murphy oddly disgusting.

Why this love of hot foul smells.

How had I never realized it before.

It could, I then considered, prove useful. There are any number of hot foul smells with which one must grapple over the course of a lifetime. If Murphy were, as he certainly appeared to be, immune to disgust in the face of hot foul smells, well, for instance, he could probably be recruited to clean Lavendar's bedding. There was no hotter, fouler smell than Lavendar's bedding, particularly when he'd made lunch of an extra-large quail's egg from Siam.

Or for that matter a small Uppal kitten.

I reluctantly released one nose-hole and sniffed. I needed to gauge Murphy's resilience. I needed to know to what limits, if limits there were, his immunity to hot foul odor reached.

There were possibly many uses to which a gift of this magnitude could be put.

There it was. My one open nose-hole caught just a hint of it on the wind of hot foul air blowing our way. It was a smell. A quiet sort of animal smell. Something yellow about the edges.

It was an undercurrent of exactly the smell of Tiki Ty's dipping.

My mouth watered with the provocation of the thought.

We had that dipping, right on our person.

Our people, I suppose, being that we were three.

The Lamb noticed my freed-up nose-hole and looked at me questioningly. I tapped the open nose-hole suggestively. She grimaced in disgust and turned to Murphy, who had no nose-holes closed. She turned back to me and wondered with her eyes. Again I tapped. Again she grimaced, but somewhat grudgingly, with an expression of deep disgust and anticipatory pain, she offered one nose-hole naked to the world.

A druggish gaze dulled her face.

She recognized it too.

Murphy slowly, very very slowly—the opposing force should not have cause to panic, thinking we were pulling out weaponry—unwrapped the bundle of remaining shrimps.

Knowing how to navigate opposing forces was a basic tenet of our training.

Slowly, so slowly, he pulled off the bakery string.

My heart ached. They were to have been saved for the return trip.

It was a sacrifice. A sacrifice to ensure that there would be a return trip.

He showed the curious crowd the shrimps, then held up a finger to indicate his trick wasn't over, that the best was yet to come. Showboating now a bit, Murphy dug around in his satchel. He made a whole act of pretending what he sought was missing. He scratched his head, he furrowed his brow. He moved his mouth in a confused fashion.

For a moment I believed that the dipping had in fact gone missing.

My heart tore asunder.

The dipping was produced!

And my heart celebrated for the split second between my realizing the dipping was not lost and my realizing that *everyone* was more accomplished at stage-acting than I.

I would require a mirror and some privacy, I decided. I would hone my craft. I would stay up, nights, to Lavendar's grumbling fury and my own health's detriment to win the next role, the best Assignment, the adoration of the viewing public.

The crowd leaned in. Yellow dipping. It was certainly thought provoking.

Murphy plucked a single shrimp from the shrimp vat, and held it up between his index finger and thumb for the crowd's examination, as though he were performing a magic trick or sleight-of-hand. He dipped, very gently, the perfect pearlescent creature into the dipping, getting just enough coated in all the right places.

Dipping is like perfuming, you know. There are points upon the shrimp that most effectively carry the flavor.

Then, in his element and with the crowd's complete cooperation, Murphy paced to and fro before the front lines, peering deep into the faces of its many heads. Finally he stopped.

The head he stopped in front of was a tremendously attractive female head.

The Lamb and I both noticed this at once.

If the stakes of this particularly attractive female head's approving of Murphy's offering weren't so high, we might have protested. We might have ripped the dip-coated shrimp from his fingers and popped it into one or the other of our own mouths, spitting only the shellacked tail bits at the lovely if not a bit bovine-expressioned head. We might have then given Murphy's foot a righteous stomping upon and turned tail and flounced away, tossing our hairs behind us.

That would give him something to remember us by.

Indeed.

I huffed slightly.

However. The stakes were high, and Murphy had chosen, and we and the crowd both held our breaths and waited.

The mouth opened. The shrimp was inserted. There was considered chewing, and nodding, and an overdone, to my mind, smacking of lush red lips, and then smiling and a bit of, to my thinking, hyperbolic moaning.

The crowd eagerly formed a line. They had never had anything like it. They'd loved so long this particular taste on their lamb and kebobs, but they did not always crave such gamey meats. They suffered some from cholesterol woes. The synthetic meats just weren't the same. They'd never considered shrimps. Never considered a simple dipping. How did one even?

And could one dip vegetables?

Would we like some champagne?

I dipped and Murphy fed. Many hands poured fine-vintaged wines down our throats and many mouths shouted various praises and blessings. Murphy drew navigational maps for Tiki Ty's Tiki Barn for the fascinated crowd and The Lamb escaped around the periphery and through the heavy doors of the devil's playground.

# 45

**At Siam, I chose** the finest and largest quail's egg for Lavendar as we waited for the proprietor to gather Tiki Ty's ingredients.

One never, never breaks a promise to a snake.

# 46

**Odille and Rogan sat** across the booth from me.

O how they shone.

It was a little embarrassing, really. I'm sure people were looking.

I was looking.

Rogan was one of those blond-headed boys you see sometimes in a very few and unlikely seeming places: on the youth, say, of the swampier regions, who resemble sun-dappled mythical beasts when you catch glimpses of them behind the vines; or on almost-adults in the icelands and drifts, when the level of albino in each male citizen falls just enough at the cusp of adulthood to allow for the glorious yellow to shine through, rendering them useless in a snowstorm subterfuge for instance *fait accompli,* but able to take any breath away from a hundred yards easy.

Rogan took my breath away neatly. I groped him a bit under the table. I made every attempt to engage him in an uncompetitive, but athletic all the same, game of footsie. I bared my teeth into the winningest smile.

He was so fetching.

Rogan kicked at me quietly.

Odille grimaced. —You know, I could help you out.

I turned my teeth toward her. Was she proposing after all to leave me and the sun-dappled mythical beast to our furtive grappling business. Was she—

—With some products, you know? She scrutinized me deep to my pores. —It's just the coloring. It's all . . . off beam.

—Off beam? I appealed to Rogan with my most beseeching lash-lowered gaze. I tried to match his fetching aspect with an equally fetching aspect.

He grimaced now too, so the two of them appeared to have been struck by the same unpleasantness.

—Is it the eyes, I wondered.

—Something like that, Odille said, though I had directed the query just to her right. And the hair. And the skin? Something like those things.

I would have liked to object but there was no basis for argument. Something like those things in fact covered it pretty accurately.

Still.

She had invited, after all, *me* to this luncheon. Politesse at least would dictate a restraint from recounting one's guest's less compelling qualities.

—So you are some sort of cosmetics technician, I told her, dripping my voice with disdain.

—() no, not really I like to toy around with it and all.

—Then what are you really? When you're not as you say toying around? With the makeup and such.

—I'm a muse.

—Well aren't We very convinced of our feminine wiles.

Nothing like the old royal We to make a person feel slightly less smug.

—No, she really is, Rogan told me, beaming proudly. —Not only to myself. To great men. Fashion designers, you know, *artistes*.

Odille beamed back at Rogan, and then her beam spread wide enough to include me, all the way on the other side of the table.

The *wattage*!

The heat and light from Rogan and Odille beaming at one another could light and heat one of the smaller Northern territories for the remainder of its existence.

The Northern territories were probably locked in fierce battle even as we sat there over who might lay claim to Rogan and Odille and their energy-producing possibilities. Yet it was I with whom they'd chosen to lunch.

Odille had extended the invitation as I'd parted ways most recently with the Professor. I'd glowed for days, between the Puppets and the summons.

—That must be fascinating work, I conceded.

She shrugged. —Pays the bills. But Rogan is the only one I care for.

—You are then a fashion designer.

—He is an *artiste*.

—Ah.

I considered for a moment. It was worth a shot. —And you are not, I suppose, in need of—just in the interest, you know, of keeping your professional and personal lives separate—

—Odille is my muse.

Mmmm.

—Even though she muses about with so many . . . ?

—It's a constantly replenishing fountain. Fount. If you will.

I hadn't much choice. Yet. —Well if you ever find yourself—

—I won't.

—Yes then. Well.

It might have been awkward then but the two of them—the *luminosity!*—were far too pretty to allow ugliness of any sort to discolor their immediate reflective pool of glory. Instead, Odille turned her gaze upon Rogan. —Tell her about your work.

I settled back into my seat with the free time afforded the third party in such an exchange; all the hemming, the hawing, the no I shouldn'ts, the what's there to really says, the lowered gazes, the stammerings about trying to find the words, the words—

*Artistes* are the pits. It's a shame the men of their species are almost all godlike.

I penned an entry into my mental daybook. I thought I might swerve my thoughts back around to the Puppets, first, in a kind of benevolent nod to my purpose and my own work, as Rogan went on about his, and then perhaps contemplate Murphy in a vague, surface-level kind of way, and then drift—briefly!—to the Whole of Literature from which it would be relatively seamless to move along to the also very important Whole of Arts and Culture at which point the squarreling twosome across the table might be ready to chime in.

—I frame people, Rogan said.

Early I might add. I'd only just mapped out my agenda.

I hadn't even *thought* of any of the things.

No hemming. No hawing.

I looked up, flustered.

—Are you okay, Odille wondered. —You have a kind of glazed aspect.

It's the eyes.

They both nodded.

—Well, Rogan said, unconcerned then about my glazed aspect and its likely continuance. —Not just framing. I mean, of course that's just what I'm working on now. Examining the materials within which we place ourselves and others, but in a literal rather than theoretical—

—You frame people.

Rogan sighed as though he'd hoped to avoid the necessary show-and-tell routine, and turned his attentions to his companion.

—Odille?

He nodded to her and she reached down to the floor and rummaged around in what appeared to be a good-sized gunnysack. As her dark head bobbed around just at the surface of the table, I made one more attempt on Rogan.

I winked and then made—it was almost unfair, years of mirrored practice standing me in such relentlessly good stead with this particular devastating skill—liquid eyes.

He winced.

The dark head rose. She presented what one would think from the fact of the gunnysack would be several severed heads of blameless children but what in fact turned out to be an unnecessarily large wooden frame, which she had to struggle to bring just halfway up to my eyeline.

—You see, she said.

I could only meet the frame's blank gaze with one of my own.

—Of course, there's no one there yet. Rogan ran a finger along one of the frame's gnarled edges. Where had he found driftwood amongst all this gravel.

—But I've framed all kinds of people—hobos, golfers, ladies, Odille. It's an incredible effect—you'll see—once the person is fixed in there. I'm framing Odille's father now.

—Really.

Well this was an interesting development. It certainly, certainly, certainly was. It demanded thought and strength and the full measure of my powers of intellect and deduction. It then demanded *re*duction, sifting of all components, relevant or not, over an open flame. With some sauce. Some consommé?

I twirled my waitstaff finger and a small hairy man scraped over. He wasn't what I'd been expecting but he was obviously a waitstaff from the clear indications of pad and hovering pencil.

—Shrimp cocktail please. On the double.

—You want double order.

It again was not what I'd meant but he was right, how right he was. A fine waitstaff. —Yes! A double order! Quickly, now, quickly!

My blood pumped and surged as though I were a released hound with the vague but unassailable scent of hare just tickling at my generously endowed snout. There was twitching in my muscles. In my very muscles there was twitching.

—Are you okay? Odille peered at me.

It was a fine feeling. I basked and glowed. I'm quite sure I would have appeared beatific, were it not for the spasticity. If I could make myself still yet retain the glow of the bask. The more however focused I became on stilling the errant muscles, the more twitchy they became. I twitched and twitched beatifically and only was very loosely aware of the profound gazes heaped upon me from the opposite side of the table. Aware, yes—how they even in their concern and disgust put forth such glorious shine!—but only loosely. In the most loose-ish of ways did I notice their gaze, and then slightly less loosely the invasion of my periphery by the small hirsute waitstaff and then with swift and sharp clarity the sparkling cocktail glasses all filled to the rims with the pinkest and most dearly opalescent shrimps!

—Yes lady here double order the finest!

I met the waitstaff's forearms in my grasp and we shared a wonderful moment of salient appreciation, in which I thought of how I would one day pen a treatise on the healing powers of shrimp, and how it would be titled *The Leveling of the Lands—How A Shrimp Saved the World!* and how I would recognize this waitstaff on the acknowledgments page, and for that matter *all* the daily shrimp vendors, toiling in obscurity save for the acknowledging eye of those patrons who recognize that nestled within those simple exchanges lies the undiluted and indisputable Divine.

# 47

**It became difficult to enjoy** completely my shrimps.

It became quite difficult because *someone* was going berserk in his satchel.

I hate to name names.

But really.

—Are you having some sort of difficulty, Rogan asked politely.

—You don't happen to have a snake in your satchel, I asked politely back.

I was shocked when he nodded.

—You have a snake in your satchel, I asked again.

—I have Golden. Rogan opened his satchel just a bit, just enough for me to discern a slim black coil within.

Lavendar was going off his rocker.

—Golden?

—This is Golden, Rogan confirmed.

—Your snake's name is Golden. I didn't even try to disguise my disgust. What sort of name was Golden for a snake.

—What's wrong with Golden?

—Well, I began, not even knowing where to begin, finding so very much wrong with the name Golden, so very much. —It's a color, for one.

—Your snake's a color, Odille said helpfully.

I stared at her. —My snake is not a color.

—Lavender?

—Your snake's name is Lavender? Rogan laughed a little bit harder than he needed to.

—My snake's name is *Lavendar.*

As I said it, I understood the confusion. And it had simply never occurred to me that Lavendar's name could be construed as a color. When we had been introduced, properly, it had simply become his name, devoid of any other association.

—That's some kind of name for a snake, Rogan said. —Lavendar.

—Well what's Golden. I tried to regain my advantage. —He's not even gold.

—No. He's just molting. And he's a she.

—Golden?

—She's named for my father, Rogan said.

—Who passed away, Odille said helpfully.

I wished Odille would stop helping. Odille's helpfulness was unjustly limited to one side of the booth. But I saw a glimmer of hope.

—Your father's name was Golden?

—Well, he was a footballer. They called him Golden because he was so fast.

—What's fast about Golden?

—Well, like greased lightning?

Lightning is an electrical impulse, four times hotter than the surface of the sun. It needs no grease to be swift, could not even *be* greased, unless perhaps it struck a silo of petroleum jelly, in which case it would be briefly greased but no faster for it.

—What's the thing I mean, Rogan said. —Quicksand.

In fact in all likelihood grease would only slow it down.

—You want to go with quick*silver,* I said. —But do you want to think it through.

Rogan thought and indicated he did not want to stick with quicksilver.

—Liquid gold?

He had a point.

Though when I thought about it just a little more, I wasn't entirely convinced. Was gold so fast in any case. Didn't gold mostly just lie there. I would have to look into it; meanwhile, I found something else, a secondary flaw.

—But your snake is black?

Rogan lost just a touch of his luster, in my eyes and for all to see. Several people, I could sense, had stopped their staring.

Can gold tarnish? Golden Rogan tarnished there before my eyes.

I had to turn away.

Someone who resembled Binelli was passing the café window as I turned.

There are very few who resemble Binelli. But what would he be doing out.

Unless he was checking on me.

Checking on me just as I had lost my focus. I turned quickly back to my companions.

Rogan said, —She'll be quite golden when she's finished molting, more golden even than before.

He brightened right back up. —And she's quite fast besides.

Rogan's wattage after its temporary tarnish beamed brighter than before. Stirring sticks went limp in their cups. Forks screeched to a halt in their eggs. Newspapers dropped to the floor, unread.

All eyes back on Golden Rogan.

Rogan was beginning to irk me, just a touch.

—Molting, I muttered.

He nodded brightly. —I'm going outside for a cigar, he said. —Will you keep your eyes on her then please? The molting makes her just a touch skittish.

Rogan took his leave.

Odille leaned across the table at me then. —Listen, she said.

I adopted a listening posture though my mind was still a bit on the Golden issue. My listening posture is enough sophisticated however that she was confident in my attentions.

160

—I wanted to talk to you alone, just quickly. I hate to worry Rogan's mind with probably insignificant matters, right as he's preparing for a gallery show.

I gave her more of the attention. It could be a break in the case.

—Did you notice, Odille said, —anything odd about my mother, for example? When you visited?

I shoved lingering Golden scraps from my thoughts with force. I shook molting bits of Golden from my mind's eye.

—How do you mean, I said.

Holding my cards to my chest.

—She's just been odd, Odille was quite willing to continue. —Almost sometimes as if she'd been drugged. All laid out on the divan, and slow. And then suddenly quite up and active and herself.

—Hmmm.

—And my father too, Odille said.

—Really. This was some new information. I sat up straighter, and then relaxed my posture back just a bit, so as to not entice a false statement based upon my own perceived expectations.

I astound even myself sometimes with my mastery of the interrogatory arts.

—Really. I mean, he's so sharp you know. And then lately, sometimes, he's gotten a bit sluggish, a bit, I don't know, stuttery? Not like he's *stuttering*, she was quick to clarify, —he's so well-spoken, obviously, but in his *way*.

—In his way, I said. —Something in his way.

—In his movements, Odille said. —Like he's stuttering around?

—Hmmm, I said again. —And you suspect—

I let the statement hang, so as not to inform her suspicions in any way.

She was much like a cuttlefish in her eagerness to snatch bait from my hook, over and over again.

—I suspect foul play, she said, eyes shining. —I don't know what sort, but foul all the same. And so— She pulled out a carefully folded scrap of paper from her admirably well-ordered satchel, and wrote some words upon it, glancing furtively around as she did. Then she took one of the table knives and cut the paper in a very deliberate and precise way, triangulating around the words until the paper was bisected, tooth-edged.

She handed me one half.

It read, in the neatest handwriting imaginable:

You    And    Took    My

I hated to seem the fool. I hated, and continue to this day to hate seeming the fool, but I hadn't the tools with which to wrest any meaning from the note. There was so little with which to work.

—What, I said, a touch of frost creeping uninvited into my voice, —am I to do with this.

Odille seemed not to notice any hint of chill in me. She seemed excited and bright and hot and eager, though her brightness I suppose was already and always there. —Whenever we next meet again, she said, almost breathless now and darting her eyes catlike between me and the door to the café, —you are to make certain before we discuss this that it's actually me you're talking to. The two halves will fit together, making the pass-phrase whole. If it's not me—if something happens to me like to my mother and father— you'll know then, if I don't have the other half of the note. You'll do something then, won't you? It'll mean I'm in some sort of trouble.

I had to give Odille credit. She had something of a knack for subterfuge.

Not an entire knack, mind you. I displayed my vaster experience. —Should I not see the entire note then. To know what it's supposed to say.

She considered, but before she had time to consider fully, Rogan reentered the café, the candied smoke clinging to his form in a desperate cloud, unwilling to part with its godlike creator. Odille and I quickly slipped our note-halves into our respective pockets, and Rogan gave us the once-over as he slid back in next to Odille.

—Am I interrupting you ladies, he said. He knew full well he could never be an interruption—not an unwelcome interruption in any case. Ladies would halt party planning, peace talks, no less than childbirth to accept an interruption from Rogan with beatific gratitude.

Odille beamed at Rogan beatifically. —You could never be an interruption, she said, right on cue. —I just don't want to bother you with stupid sundries. While you're working, you know.

Rogan nodded. He said to me, —You see why she's such a sought-after muse.

I tried to beam and they both lowered their eyes.

I took my leave, dragging Lavendar and my light-dimming qualities from their glorious circle. It was not, I'm quite certain, just my imagination that behind me the table burned just a touch brighter, the closer I got to the door.

# 48

**Murphy had something to say** and I wished he'd say it.

An entire afternoon of Rogan and Odille and their brilliance and unwaveringly becoming aspects had tried my patience mightily.

His pockets jangled right on my last nerve.

I turned to him with brutal force.

Something large and soft but still surprising hit me square in the face.

My fury knew no bounds.

I am gifted in the area of furious invective and furious invective I hurled upon Murphy. I wondered many things about his person and his personal hygiene and his personality tics and his physical tics and his terrible terrible way with manners.

My invective he accepted with a brave face.

A brave face that crumpled far too soon into not streaming cawing tears and sobs as intended but laughter.

—It's your pillow, Murphy said, picking the offending object off the floor.

While extremely and unnaturally gifted in the area of furious invective, I have very little control of it once said invective is unleashed. It's a raw sort of gift. I am not too proud to admit it wants honing.

The new information failed to staunch the stream of invective. We both waited it out.

We thought it was over but then a few dribbling remains proved us wrong.

Then I was free to say, —What.

—It's your pillow, he said, laughing so pleased as punch. —Your pillow, he said, —that we'd left in the last place.

I had a vague recollection.

I eyed the bundle.

—But we didn't leave it, see, Murphy said triumphantly. —I snuck it in, with the rest. It occurred to me that we might never go back. It occurred to me you might want it.

Murphy's triumph is oftentimes too triumphant to bear—a raw sort of triumph that even he might admit wants honing—but there was something to it this time.

—I do want it, I said. I took it from his hands. I sniffed at it.

—It was the best one, Murphy said.

—It really, I said, —was.

# 49

There was still the matter of Tiki Ty's pocketry.

I slipped from my bed and crept from the room with such extraordinary stealth I did not even wake Lavendar, who is programmed to detect stealth and pull back the blinds on it, exposing it for the clumsy sham that it usually is.

I crept through hallways and down steps and through vast rooms of vintage surfing memorabilia and books and into the kitchen.

It was dark but not so dark that I couldn't make out a form upon one of the stools at the kitchen table, nor was it so dark that I couldn't make out a form upon the table itself, a form that resembled some manner of cake.

The form and I stood off.

The form upon the stool, that is. The cakelike form could do nothing but be itself and emit a weak odor that my trained nose determined to be rum-raisin.

The form upon the stool lost the standoff as it could not help but do.

—Finley, the form whispered with the voice of The Lamb.

I deigned not to answer. We both knew it was I. Who else could cut such a silhouette.

I strode imperiously to the table. I surveyed the domain. I had been quite correct; the cake was rum-raisin, and had been ravaged by a fork, which was held guiltily in one of The Lamb's small paws.

There were crumbs in her curls.

She motioned with the fork to another stool. —Would you care for some cake, she said dispiritedly.

I could not answer with any conviction.

I hadn't recollection upon which I could call of previous dealings with rum-raisin cake. Though dealings I must have had, at some time, with the smell so easily identifiable.

I cast my mind back through the cakes course at Battersea. Certainly, among all those cakes, I must have sampled a rum-raisin!

But it simply wasn't true.

Would I care then for some cake.

I sat, agitated. I watched the cake for a moment. It gave no indication, one way or the other, of being tasty.

I hated to expose a not-knowing but I had to ask. —Is it tasty, I said to The Lamb.

It pained her to admit it, I could see, but her feelings toward the cake could not be denied, even though a denial might very well have resulted in more cake for her.

—It is, The Lamb said, —quite tasty.

She handed me her fork, tines politely facing away.

I chipped off a cluster of crumbs. The Lamb grabbed back the fork. —No, you have to get some raisin too, she said, very angry. She stabbed at the cake, secured a large piece with raisins bursting from every angle, and handed it back to me, shaking with fury but still politely switching her grip so that the tines would not stab my grasping hand.

I ate the bite.

The Lamb was right. It was quite tasty. It was a bit of a taste explosion. There was rum and there were raisins, and they completed one another in a way I had not expected but in such a way that I suddenly could not imagine them apart.

How had I never known?

The Lamb stared with utter dejection at my reaction to the cake and stood without speaking and padded across the kitchen to the drawer and fetched herself another fork.

We had a nice time then for a while, me and The Lamb, eating the rum-raisin.

After some part of the nice time, which we'd been spending in comfortable chewy silence but for the occasional fork scrape, The Lamb asked me what was I doing, creeping around the Tiki Barn.

She had been so honest with me, about the cake. I repaid her in kind. —Have you ever, I said, —noticed Tiki Ty's pockets.

She nodded until her mouth was cleared enough of rum-raisin to speak, eyes wide. —You know it's funny you ask, she said. —I have noticed. I noticed just recently, she said, crumbs spilling everywhere and her hair neatly catching them all.

When the cake was finished, she would have a nice dessert course of it right there in her hair.

—I'm going to find out about them, I said. —Learn a little more. Maybe see if we might not get a tailor on board to fashion some for us.

She nodded. —An Italian you were thinking?

—I was thinking so. But, I took my mouthful and then stabbed the empty fork into the air to punctuate my next point, —the Italians are perhaps just too disruptive.

—Do you think, she said. She rolled a raisin delicately around between her top and bottom front teeth. —Maybe we could find a less disruptive one, who still could tailor?

—I thought of that, I said. —But then I thought, would a moderately Italian Italian tailor so well as perhaps a fully Thai Thai?

It had been something I'd been mulling over and not quite decided. I was pleased to find an unexpected sounding board in The Lamb. I continued my thought process. —Because it seems to me, and do correct me by all means if I'm wrong, that many garments are made in Thailand.

The Lamb nodded and I sensed clicking in her head. —You're

quite right, she said, —and that would make a lot of sense, wouldn't it, and so simple. I'm surprised we didn't think of it before.

The Lamb was stealing a bit of my thunder, catching some sort of connection at which I had not yet arrived. I racked my brain over a forkful of rum-raisin. I ransacked my available information on Thailand. There seemed to be little beyond what I had already said aloud.

I felt moderately doleful but it was cleared up with the burst of an exceptionally plump raisin in my bite. I would share my thunder with The Lamb as she had shared her rum-raisin cake with me.

—Think of what, I said.

—Tiki Ty, she said. —It's all so obvious now. That's why he's got such pockets. I bet he could make them for us all.

—He's not Italian, I said. It sounded hollow and slow even to my own ears. I knew there was something quite faulty with my response but I didn't for the life of me know what it was.

The Lamb knew. She looked at me with something akin to pity. —Of course he's not, she said. —He's Thai.

—He's Thai?

—Tiki *Ty?* What did you expect he might be.

Something dawned on me much slower than it had any right to. —He is then, I said very carefully, —Tiki *Thai?*

The nice time The Lamb and I were having was very much over. The Lamb was laughing and spraying precious rum-raisin everywhere. Her look was less akin to and more awash now in pity.

—Poor Finley, she said through her cake and her mirth and her glee and her crumbs. —Poor Finley.

The rum-raisin cake was pretty much finished anyway. I could stalk from the room without at least that regret.

# 50

## Theory No. 3 Regarding The Lamb's Freakish Intelligence

She has none.

No intelligence, freakish or otherwise.

The Lamb is simply an excellent actor.

I'm not saying there's anything wrong with that. I'm not trying to indicate any malicious malfeasance on the part of The Lamb. I'm accusing The Lamb of neither willful self-misrepresentation nor improper use of her License for Stage and Screen™ card. I am simply saying that what sometimes would appear to be freakish intelligence is in fact only Acting.

It's really quite obvious.

Notice: The Lamb takes part in a conversation. An extremely smart joke is told. As everyone is saying, Hey, Finley, great one! The Lamb laughs the hardest. She gets it.

Smart.

Notice this as well: Everyone stews, chin to palm, over a problem. Some doodle the loose ends onto paper and try every which way to force a connection. Some jingle their pockets and keep a serious thinking face. Some pace feverishly back and forth, back and forth, fitting together unfitting pieces from a room-sized factory-recalled jigsaw puzzle.

There is no hope.

It's beyond reason and logic.

And then . . . someone starts to speak and then who but The Lamb starts to speak at exactly the same moment, saying the exact same words, only half a split-second after.

Each word.

One half of one split-second after. After the sentence is spoken and echoed—an echo so slight, hardly anyone even notices it wasn't all in unison now wasn't it and have a great day—everyone laughs and gives pats on the back all around and isn't it: —The Lamb, Finley, great minds think alike, and: —How did you two come up with, and: —Isn't it funny how it came, like a lightning bolt, to both of them at once.

Funny.

Now all I'm saying is, I'm not an excellent actor, myself.

This is a fact to which I'm certainly at this point willing to admit.

Might others admit their own facts.

Might others not try to be absolutely everything.

Might others give others of us, perhaps, a break.

That's all I'm saying.

# 51

I left The Lamb in the kitchen with her rollicking good time and her rum-raisin remains, and stalked right into the room of Tiki Ty— who I simply could not rename in my mind according to the new information, no matter his origins, and so who shall not be re-named throughout the account for is not consistency as impor-tant at least as exactitude—and turned on his light switch, and demanded of his sleeping form an explicit explanation of his won-drous pocketry.

Tiki Ty blinked.

—And I'd like my note, I said, —as well.

Tiki Ty blinked.

I foraged through his things, which were quite all about, quite ripe for the foraging in fact, so greatly did they resemble in their lying-all-aboutness things that had already been foraged, several times, by several different interested parties.

I found my note and brought the bottoms into which it had been tucked to his bed.

I presented Tiki Ty with said bottoms.

I waited.

Tiki Ty presently blinkered off the top layers of his sleep and gave me a thorough tutorial in savage pocketry. He would *yes* help me savagely pocket my own clothing, quite beyond the few shabby pockets I already owned. He *yes* was quite Thai and really had I not known this, all this time. And what had I thought then was his name. And, all right, that was understandable, he supposed, and even lovely in its way, and perhaps he would have it officially changed in the record books and he wondered then if he could go back to sleep.

All business completed to our mutual satisfaction, he could.

# 52

Everyone was sullen and out-of-sorts. Everyone, perhaps, blamed me.
No one said it outright.

The Lamb held her stomach with an aspect of showy indigestion and in a demonstration of admirably calculated foresight had
painted her eyelashes long so as to better glare up at me through
them.

Tiki Ty yawned and made noises regarding hours of sleep and
interruption of sleep and sleep's regenerative life-giving properties
and though he'd had no recourse to the eyelash paint, his eyelashes
were naturally quite dark and long and stuck somewhat sidewise in
a way that accentuated his accusing sidewise glances.

His accusing sidewise glances were in fact so effective that after
a while I noticed The Lamb had become more fixated on Tiki Ty
than on me, and was peering up steadily through her dark thrush
of lash at his eyes rather than mine.

I shared The Lamb's indigestion though it did not behoove me to
clutch at my stomach and cast about accusing glances, there being
no sorry shamed soul to stand lonely at their receiving end. And having such pale eyelashes besides, so that peering up through them
amounted to nothing so much as peering up through a vague beige

netting and causing in general a collective distaste rather than arias of apologia and the bowing and scraping for which one would hope.

It occurred to me that at least The Lamb's plight was not unduly a result of my participation in the rum-raisin fandango. If I had not in fact participated in the rum-raisin fandango, chances were that The Lamb's plight would be considerably more dire. It occurred to me that I was due perhaps a thanking from The Lamb, for bearing some of the brunt of the rum-raisin fandango myself, thus sparing her digestive system the full weight of cake to which it would almost certainly have been subjected had I not made my entrance at the exact moment I did. It occurred to me that it would be perfectly appropriate for me to do some sidewise or upward or otherwise peering of my own, at least toward The Lamb, but of course for reasons already mentioned it would prove a futile and worthless endeavor and, as it were, my system in its delicate state preferred a more straightforward stare right then.

I did give it a little try all the same.

It was indeed futile and worthless, and elicited even a little shriek from The Lamb, who had not been expecting such sudden bald exposure to my eyes.

Though Tiki Ty perhaps enjoyed a momentary reprieve from The Lamb's hard gaze, and it occurred to me that this in itself might restore me to his good graces.

Too much inner occurring, however, coupled with all the peering, upset my stomach's terse equilibrium and I retired to the Tiki Barn proper, where I thought I might find a slim tawdry volume of vintage California noir within whose pages I might lose myself until things set themselves to rights.

The glare in the Tiki Barn was startling.

The Tiki Barn is a place that seems quite bright and airy until actual outside bright and air make an unexpected entrance and expose the perceived airy brightness for the sham that it is. The perceived bright and air then slink to the supply closet, which enjoys a brief, though of course false, glow and aridity for a few days until the forgetful phantoms roam back out into the more open and impressive venue for their impressions.

We are no less forgetful. We take these petty imposters each time at face value until—Such bright! Such breeze! Such glory as to indicate, if one were a manner of holy-rolling zealot, which I am not, that some sort of Reckoning or Coming or Ascension were taking place and feasts should be prepared and vestments cast off or taken up depending on one's own brand of zealotry and bodies should be lain by a low wide river or dipped straightaway into a low wide river, again depending on the course one's zealotry takes.

I made out a form in the door from which the glow emanated.

Seemed to emanate.

The form, of course, being in the door, became part and parcel with the presumed actual source of the bright and the air, which was of course the sun and the atmosphere. It was an effect, was all, causing the form to appear to glow and breeze.

Then the form stepped forward and the glow moved forward with it.

It was Rogan.

O the brilliance!

I walked to and he walked fro. We engaged in a bit of mirror ballet. A bit of fencing and feinting as I drew near and he drew far, I drew right and he drew left.

A blessed miscalculation on his part brought us face-to-face.

—Rogan, I said, more breathlessly than I intended.

—Finley, he said, short of breath himself but for one could be fairly certain a very different reason.

Though he maintained an excellent form, Rogan was perhaps just a touch out of shape?

—Have you come for cake, I said, —because I'm afraid the rum-raisin is quite well done for.

—Cake, he said. —Why would I come for cake?

—Well the cake is very good, I said. —Was very good, I said. —When it was.

He perhaps had never sampled rum-raisin either. He was perhaps as in the dark to its charms as I had been, mere hours hence. If only there had been more cake, I thought, I could introduce the glowing Rogan to the bursting rum-raisin and once the inevitable combustion of perfection died down, I would contentedly bask in the afterglow.

It was not alas an option.

—I just wanted to see the surfing memorabilia, Rogan said. —Specifically the Woodies.

—The which, I said.

—The Woodies, Rogan said. —The old ones. The wooden ones. The classics.

—Mmmm yes, I said.

I darted my eyes about the Barn a bit, trying to find something other than walls and roof beams and books that might fit the old/wooden description.

—*Surfboards,* Rogan said. —The *Woodies.*

—Of course, I said. —The surfboards. Well there are vintage surfing memorabilias all about so you can perhaps take a look and find something like that.

I considered something.

—You know, I said, —you are not to *take* the surfing memorabilias to use as wood for frames.

—I'm not taking anything, Rogan said, rolling his eyes more exaggeratedly than seemed to me necessary. He was after all someone who bent wood to his will. There was no cause to take such offense.

Such offense though he took. He huffed and snorted. He resembled a great golden cow, stamping and hoofing and eye-rolling. He resembled a great golden ox, rather, unaware of oncoming slaughter, impervious to mortality at the hands of cowhands and cowboys and herders and butchers. He basked in his bright golden glow and felt free to grimace and lick and kick his hooves against the lovely wood grain, stirring up sawdust.

The kitchen door slammed open and Tiki Ty appeared, a bloody apron wrapped loosely around his garb and brandishing a blade.

—Finley, he said. —Why so much banging?

Rogan's mortality caught swiftly up to him. His kicking stopped but I made a long pointed look toward the offending foot, for Tiki Ty's sake and for, by proxy, my own.

Tiki Ty looked at the foot, glanced cursorily at the attached limb and torso, not seeming even slightly blinded by Rogan's light, and backed back into the kitchen.

I was mightily redeemed.

We maintained our posture for some time, Rogan and I.

The air around him was warmer than the air away from him.

My eyes streamed great golden tears.

# 53

**I applied** my gigantic aviator-style sunglasses.

I enjoy and excel at feats of silence, but I also wondered.

—Is Odille then not with you, I said.

Had they fought.

Had he left her struggling over a silver tray of meats in her gilded prison of an ancestral home. Was she dripping salty tears, even now, onto the meats, her woe only enhancing the delicate flavors, so that those finally served would wonder after her special recipe.

Odille's special recipe of heartbreak and inconsolable aloneness.

My mouth watered and my eyes dried, though a fine foggy residue remained on my enormous lenses. I beamed at Rogan's fine foggy form.

Rogan squinted, as though I were the one emanating a dangerous ferocity of bright. He looked at the door as he said, —No, she's right behind me.

On cue, a hint of persimmon infiltrated the Tiki Barn, followed shortly by Odille.

O the grandeur.

The largesse.

The unfortunate gait of an oversized beauty who'd stopped for cocktails at the cocktail stand positioned conveniently nearby the Tiki Barn bookshop and vintage surfing memorabilia mausoleum, in a stroke of marketing genius on the part of Tiki Ty, who understood that a person's purchasing power increases at levels akin to their alcohol consumption and who, while maintaining strict unwavering faith in the quality of goods available for perusal at the Tiki Barn, felt no harm or shame in lubricating the way for his good and fine patrons.

That is to say, Odille seemed just a little bit drunk.

Though the persimmon smell, besides being intoxicating, acted as an excellent masker of other smells like drinking.

That is to say, Odille did not smell of drink. Odille smelled only of persimmons. Persimmons such as could make one, if one were the swooning type, which I admittedly am, swoon.

When I had myself picked up from the floor unaided mind you by any helping hand and dusted off sawdust and wood stain, several persons had been added to the room.

Two persons had been added. They had the aspect of interns—harried and weak and thin and bedraggled and in scuffed-up boots.

—Who may I say is calling, I said with severe politeness. Let it never be said I am no friend of the intern. Let it never conversely be said, however, that I look kindly upon their kind.

—They're just Rogan's interns, Odille said. —Art students, you know. Never mind them.

I was already not minding them—though on a deeper level I minded them of course very much simply for their common-to-every-intern simpering ways—because I was minding instead a dark flash of Binelli down the Oversized Book row.

Whether in the interest of disinterested evaluation or vast and glorious promotional possibilities or scalding dressing-down, I was being observed.

My spine adjusted into the being-observed position, which was to say, quite straight. I was then in a position to peer down at the interns, though still up at the tremendous Odille.

Were the elder Uppals so disproportionately enormous. Whence this giantess.

I made a note to better observe heights and lineages.

I made a note to remember to make that note slightly later, when paper was available, and to add to that note the better making of frequent observant notes on the readily available paper I would make an addendum to the note to procure and then have with me at all times so notes could be made and so the report would then stop being so gratingly tedious to reassemble from memory, of which mine is, have no doubt, fine, but really. One has hardly the time.

—Don't trouble the things, I said firmly to the interns and dismissed them thus.

They did not scatter.

Nor did they slink away, bruised.

Like unripe green apples, they held their skin well.

—I'd like to examine the Oversized Books, Odille said. —The interns may escort me.

Rogan nodded and the interns took Odille by either elbow and led their large charge down the row.

I saw a shadow of Binelli down the Most Dangerous Waves aisle.

I said, —And what was it then you were after.

—Woodies, said Rogan, straining to find the source of peripheral disruption that was Binelli.

—Woodies, I said, —would in all likelihood be found in the loft area.

I gestured toward the steps.

Rogan was bright in most areas but dull in the most incomprehensible others and distractible as a marmot. He forgot quite neatly the phantom Binelli and took the stairs two at a time.

I enjoyed the ascending scenery until his ascension was complete and then I strode with purpose down Oversized.

Odille was staring at the shelf closest to her eye level, not appearing to scan the titles at all but in a rather blank manner, as though she'd no real interest in Oversized Books after all but perhaps had feigned the interest in order to create the conditions for a private conversation between her and me.

I stood beside her and stared into the shelf.

The interns were at the end of the row, deep in inconsequential conversation.

—Shall we, I said, —activate the pass-phrase.

Odille looked ceilingward. —Must we, she said.

I was unforeseeably disappointed. I had carried around my jagged little orphan fragment with growing excitement for the moment it would be reunited with its twin and its broken language healed and revealed.

—Well, I said, —it was at your direction. In the first place.

I felt hot about the scalp.

—So yes, I said, before she could let escape whatever words had pried open her great garish lips in the pursuit of freedom, —we must.

Odille let out a deep sigh and the interns glanced our way.

I held them off with a stern stare. Not my sternest. My sternest could collapse an intern to ash. A mild version got the job done neatly. The interns slunk entirely from the row.

Odille rummaged about in her satchel, which she must have had custom-made, so perfectly proportioned was it to her tremendous frame.

I gripped my own paper more tightly than intended between my thumb and index finger.

Odille produced her own jagged scrap and with an almost sense of transcendence did I bring my paper to meet hers.

Her paper said:

YOU    AND    TOOK    MY

My paper still said:

YOU    AND    TOOK    MY

182

Our papers together, jags coming together in no sort of perfect way, read:

YOU   YOU   AND   AND   TOOK   TOOK   MY   MY

and I wept at least three hot tears and closed my fist around my scrap.

—That, I said, —is not correct. Not in the least, Odille, correct.

Odille smiled wanly. —Of course not, she said, digging around some more in her satchel. —It's just, I use these all the time, and sometimes I forget who got what half, and the satchel, it's so messy, and, she lowered her voice a notch against prying intern ears, —I am, I have to admit, just a tiny bit drunk.

I nodded. This had been clear.

—So do you mind, Odille said, —very much. It's just all bits of paper and pieces of wood and wax-papered meats in here. It could take ages. Can we do it the next time?

—I suppose, I said, —that would be fine.

Never mind my freshly fogged sunglasses.

Her satchel *was* quite large, and *quite* messy on this occasion. I could hardly begrudge her her drunkenness. My feelings might have been hurt that she recycled pass-phrases, if I cared about that sort of thing, which naturally I did not, and my curiosity would certainly kill me slowly as to the lettered secret of my paper-bit's twin, but these inconveniences were no greater than inconveniences almost constant to my line of work, inconveniences in fact inconceivable to most, which I bore with valor almost every waking minute of every day.

So, yes, I supposed it would be fine to welcome a fresh gnawing voice into the brutal chorus. The alto section was weak, in any case, and one never does, does one, know but that a new tone in a thin octave might pull the whole bloody cacophonous riot into harmony.

I took my leave.

# 54

**After checking on the status** of my hairline in the basin mirror for a few blessedly uninterrupted minutes, I remembered the other, infinitely more important note still in my satchel. How long had it been since Battersea. I berated myself for the unconscionable delay in unfolding Kiki B's missive, for taking such juvenile excitement in pass-phrases and oxen, golden though they be, and letting what might be an urgent message molder in the satchel.

And what if Lavendar had gotten to it.

Snakes are not overly fond of paper, it's true, but Lavendar has been known to consume all manner of product, paper or otherwise, to the taste of which snakes are not predisposed.

Neither here nor there. The note was intact. I unfolded it.

## 55

**The Contents of Kiki B's Second Note:**

There once was a one person who
Knew all that she knew was untrue
She fell asleep in her head
When she woke up instead
Of being one one, she was two.

# 56

Kiki B's note was quite a disappointment.

# 57

—Do you remember, said Murphy, —the Baseball Assignment.

We were lazing about Wax & Leashes, an area of the Tiki Barn that, despite the pornographic implications of its name, was a sunny colorful area, plastics gleaming amongst all the wood.

—I do not—

—How could you not.

—Would you let me finish, I said.

—You were speaking very slowly, he said. —I thought you had done.

—I choose, I said, —my words with care.

I had recently in fact been dressed down by Binelli, and not in the good and fun and natural way one would like a dressing-down to proceed but rather in the manner of Binelli angrily suggesting that I choose my words with care sometimes and not unleash invective as if I suffered from a certain disorder of the central nervous system that makes its victims unleash invective, or did I perhaps suffer from that disorder and how sorry he was to not be more sensitive to my handicap and did I perhaps require the services of special doctors or perhaps a rest, some time off, some chamomile-flower tea with honey and perhaps a nice long soak in the tub.

—Since when, Murphy said, —do you choose your words with care.

—Since my tub, I said with dignity.

—So you do remember.

—I do not wish, I said, —to revisit the past. The past is of no use to me.

—Well there's the *past* past, which I suppose is of no use to you, *supposably,* Murphy said, —but the past *since* that past, I just don't really see the harm.

—I don't see the good, I said.

—Suppos*ed*ly, I said.

—But do you remember, Murphy said, ignoring my grammar lesson, —the great green grasses. The chalk they'd use to whiten the base path. That marvelous machine they'd spin to brush the dust from the white.

I did remember. There'd been a scheme afoot at the ballpark and it had all been terrifically intoxicating. I remembered when the baseball men would come out of a dewy morning and toss their balls about and give one another the razz about their haircuts or wives or behavior of the evening prior. They'd throw lazy pitches at the home plate and the crack of the bat, far from startling, was a sort of familiar putting the day to rights.

—You do then, Murphy said, watching closely my face.

—I do.

—Good, Murphy said.

—I remember everything, I said.

He peered at me so.

—You remember about as much as a little fish, Murphy said, —but it's a start.

# 58

**I had not ordered** the fish but the little bits of fish I tasted from Odille's plate were fine.

Look at Odille and I, friends, fast friends, sharing bites from one another's plates!

Though Odille did not take bites from my plate. Admittedly, when I caught Odille eyeballing my shrimps in her seductive long-lashed way, I put a quick protective hand up between Odille and the platter, as a child might shield her in-class assignment from a seductive long-lashed side-glancing cheater.

A child, faced with Odille's cheating eyes, might turn over her test, if truth be told.

Especially might turn over *his* test.

I was not however a child and the shrimps were fine that great gray afternoon, and the portions were not so big. It was practical to keep one's shrimps to oneself.

Odille if she so loved shrimps might have ordered a small platter for herself, as a side course.

Our lopsided sharing did not create the atmosphere of awkwardness about the table that it might have, such fast friends were we being on that day. The atmosphere indeed was festive, with Odille resplendent in a great caftan the dozy color of bruised tuberose, and necklaces upon necklaces, of wood and bone and hammered metals, strung time and time again about her neck, and a splash of coral balm staining her gigantic lips.

Indeed it was a fine time. Odille was in a conspiratorial way. —Rogan, have you noticed, has had umpteen secret errands to run.

I hadn't noticed. I stroked Lavendar through the heavy rucksack material of his satchel and he stretched out like a cat for a midday scratch.

It would behoove me, I noted mentally—yes, mentally, again, for had I paper? I had not paper—to notice Rogan's comings and goings with a touch more alacrity.

—O? I said, and Odille nodded, resembling quite out of nowhere nothing so much as an adolescent bull, all head, an exaggerated nod not entirely in keeping with the formidable grace of her bearing.

—I can't believe you hadn't noticed, Odille said, as though tracking a rogue Rogan was of as much interest to me as to her.

Which indeed it was, but Odille couldn't know that. It was perfectly in keeping however with the close friendship Odille and I were sharing—yes!—right there at the diner, sharing food from one another's forks and gossiping like the elderly over our friends' and relations' every movement.

—He gets a furtive look when he's about to go, Odille said, —as though he's preparing his excuse.

She laughed, throwing her head back, which would come off as awkward if the head-thrower had not been in fact Odille, on whom the gesture seemed perfectly natural.

*She threw her head back and laughed!* a biography of Odille would one day say, and the critics would lambast the author for cliché; only characters in novels and actors in theatricals throw their heads back laughing without coming off spastic or lunatic or autistic.

Though that last is not right. The autistic prefer to stay quite still, to my knowledge.

—I keep thinking, she said, —I should let him give me one. An excuse, I mean. He must spend so much time coming up with them.

—Are you not bothered, I said.

—Bothered, she said. —Why would I be bothered?

Odille enjoyed an obscene surety regarding Rogan's affections. As perhaps her very *best* friend, I agreed with my whole heart that Rogan's attentions could not possibly stray elsewhere—where would they possibly go—but also in my role as absolute best friend in perhaps the world, I had to also keep at least a toe dipped in the wellsprings of possibility.

—With the sneaking, I said. —If he were just going to the studio, he'd tell you, right. If he were gathering up wooden things to break or gathering rats for the snake—

—Or finding leaves to rake? Odille said.

—I don't follow. I made a mental note, however, to investigate Rogan's raking habits and to conduct exhaustive searches of leaf piles in the area.

Odille patted the air around my hair affectionately. —I'm just joking. Of course he's not doing those things. Raking. Can you imagine.

She was quite correct. Leaves, amidst so much gravel! I made a mental note to investigate instead the habits of fast friends—the jokes they make, the word games they play, et cetera.

Odille leaned in very close to my shrimps but it was to conspire rather than to steal as it turned out so I leaned in quite close to her face in return, and she pulled back just a notch or two. —I'm sorry, she said, —it's your eyes. I can't be quite so close; you understand.

I did understand and it was a testament to our bosom friendship that she could say such a thing to me and know we would yet remain friends, though it smarted, yes, I admit it smarted.

I pulled back a notch myself but could think of nothing repugnant in her aspect or bearing to blame it on aloud and so make her smart back.

Odille used a stagey whisper to span the now not inconsiderable distance between us. —I suspect he's gearing up to ask me to be . . . betrothed.

This was unexpected.

Though I couldn't tell if it should have been unexpected.

It was proving complicated to reconcile my own professional purposes with the notion that Rogan and Odille might be up to something so pedestrian. A thing so pedestrian would simply never in all the certainly thousands of tiny pistons of possibility blowing and clanging in my brain have occurred to me.

I felt slightly ill all through my thinking and feeling apparati.

—Do you know something, Odille said. She grasped my two hands in her two hands across the table and fairly shook them. —You have a strange look about you. Is that not it at all then? Is there something else?

I shook my hands from her grasp and mopped at my forehead and rubbed at my temples and blinked my eyes until they cleared of the great gray cloud that had passed before them. Odille was pained of face, peering so earnestly and troubled. Everything shook off from me at once and I threw my head back in as near an approximation of her earlier gesture as I could manage and laughed.

Odille, rather than commenting unfavorably on the cut of my throat or the severe point of certain of my teeth or the profoundly disturbing sound I emitted, threw her head back and laughed with me.

We had a good long laugh, during the course of which we decided, mutually but without having to speak, that of course Rogan would be requesting her delicate many-ringed hand in marriage, to have and to hold and et cetera.

Such was the depth of our friendship.

At the end of our laugh Odille reached into her neat-again satchel and pulled triumphantly from it a jagged scrap of paper. —Shall we, she said.

The slightly ill feeling returned, just in a short wave. I had, after our failed pass-code attempt, crumpled up the worthless bit and stuck it deep inside Lavendar's satchel.

I have already reviewed Lavendar's propensity for paper.

—I know it's you, I said to Odille.

I grasped the hands I'd dropped so unceremoniously earlier and, surprisingly, she squeezed mine back.

**Odille drove me** back to the Tiki Barn in a golfing cart we borrowed from a fleet of several waiting outside the diner. Odille drove quite proficiently and with ease, allowing me to gaze out upon the gravel with not a care in the world.

A lazy blimp floated soundlessly overhead, like the firmest cloud you could imagine.

# 60

—Okay, so, Murphy said, as though he were finally getting around to the salient point of a conversation in progress, though no conversation had been in progress until he spoke, —what do you think is the *deal* with this Investigation.

The Lamb, kneeling upon a long wooden surfboard and care fully trimming the tips off her curls with indescribably tiny scissors, expressed not even the remotest intention of engaging in this topic.

It was fascinating to watch, these trimmings.

I would have responded myself had I any idea what Murphy was talking about.

I leaned comfortably up against a long wooden surfboard that was propped up in one corner of the loft. The Woodies section, as it turned out.

Woodies having turned out to be the long wooden surfboards upon which The Lamb, Murphy, and I were reclined in various postures of relaxation.

My posture was perhaps more comfortable than either The Lamb's or Murphy's, aided as it was by my rescued pillow. I alternated between watching The Lamb trim her tips and the examination of a photograph hung on one of the loft's walls.

I intended no irony when I reported earlier that The Lamb's

trimmings were fascinating to watch, though I see now how the statement could have been misconstrued.

Her trimmings *were* fascinating. The care, the *care* she took to separate each ringlet into its own regal entity, twirling each majestic curl around a surprisingly elongated right index finger. The absorption with which she examined for splits, the deftness of her sudden snips.

Had The Lamb always been left-handed.

Or was it only with scissors.

—I mean, Murphy said, —I finished my Assignment ages ago, really, just finalized things up today, like something to fill a couple hours of my time, and The Lamb, hers—

I had no interest in entertaining discussion of The Lamb's Assignment, nor, now that the topic of her Assignment had come up, interest anymore in The Lamb's dexterous grooming.

I turned my attentions back to the photograph. It depicted a diner counter, nothing fancy, at which were seated, one could assume by their general raffish appearance, et cetera, to be a group of young adults. Despite having their backs to the camera, and despite their uniformity of hair—which was to the last much like Kiki B's, mangy and dirtily blond—they appeared to be a group of mixed gender. I could tell this by their various legs, some of which were shapely and dimpled and others of which were knobby and furred, and also by their various bottom-wear, some of which were the long sort of swimming shorts that come in and out of favor at incalculable intervals and at least one of which was an obscenely short skirt. But what interested me most was that each sweatshirted back bore across its breadth, though some letters of each were obscured by floppy hoods hanging at rangy angles, the word SURFBIRDS.

Where had I seen this.

It played at the very tip of my brain.

—And you, Murphy said, —I mean what's up with Puppets? I half feel like he just set you loose on some poor unsuspecting guy's retirement project just to—

—Professor's, I said, quite by reflex but unwittingly launching myself into precisely the conversation I had been studiously and successfully avoiding for so long.

—What?

—Professor. Not some guy, I said.

—Fine, Murphy said, shaking his head as though a bee had just landed there and was causing not so much fear but aggravation. —But I mean, it seems like you're not really Investigating—

—I'm Investigating right now, I said.

It was true, too, though I'll be the first to admit I'd said it simply to quiet Murphy's own private investigation, having evidently exhausted his Assignment's possibilities and in need of Something of Interest.

I was Investigating the Woodies.

Or, more aptly, I was Investigating the possible causes of Rogan's itch to visit the Woodies section, which had come out of the blue and apropos of nothing.

Apropos of nothing I could yet discern, would be perhaps more correct.

And I was Investigating by immersing myself into the scene of the itch. I had brought the pillow, even, in case the Investigation should bump up against bedtime. It was not my fault the others had followed me up. I hadn't set out to host a party, or even a small get-together; I'd not brought snacks. I'd ordered no entertainment.

If Murphy thought I wasn't Investigating, he was a worse Investigator than I'd thought.

Perhaps why Binelli had Assigned him a throwaway.

—What are you Investigating, Murphy said.

—My Assignment, I said. Though it was true I was at the moment more concerned with the photograph on the wall of the Surfbirds. I felt an answer was imminent, an answer that might go beyond a temporary inherent curiosity in vintage surfing curiosos but lean toward something greater.

A memory even.

—Your Investigation, Murphy said, —is hanging up on that wall.

—I feel, I said, trembling just a bit, —on the verge of a memory.

Murphy jangled just a bit about the pockets.

—Or I *felt,* I clarified, —on the verge of a memory.

Murphy jangled infuriatingly.

Why did Lavendar only rage when they were actually spilled when the jangling itself was so infuriating.

—It has passed, I said, —due to interruption.

—Maybe I can help, Murphy said. —Maybe we—

He turned toward The Lamb, who had managed to extricate herself from any danger of helpful involvement or continued conversation by neatly disappearing, leaving only a lonely heap of hairs upon the board where she'd knelt, as if some myopic shark had mistaken her neither plump nor sleek figure on the surfboard for a delicious snack, then spit out the split bits.

—Maybe we, said I, meaning Murphy, —should take our cue from The Lamb and take our leave.

Murphy stood and extracted his hands from his pockets. He offered me one.

I declined his offer, though I suspected the hand in question was warm.

—I am still Investigating, I said, —whether or not it's apparent to an untrained eye.

I turned my attentions back to the photograph and maintained my gaze until Murphy had taken his leave. Then I leaned back on my pillow and closed my eyes.

I am expert in feats of endurance; I would wait the memory out.

# 61

**Sure enough, it came** to me in the night.

The Surfbirds were minor but recurring characters from a California noir novel I had recently enjoyed.

The photograph was a still from a film they'd subsequently shot.

Upon closer inspection, the photograph in fact expressed its origins in minute writing along the bottom left-hand edge of the mat, though this I did not notice until I had already had my revelation.

It was a grievous, though I will say not entirely unexpected, disappointment.

# 62

**As was The Lamb's play.**

Of course we all had to attend.

Of course we all had to not only attend but send along flowers ahead to her dressing room.

Of course we had also to suffer The Lamb's histrionics in the hours prior, when her hair would not curl in exactly the girlish way she'd been rehearsing, and she lashed out with accusations of sabotage at whomever had made the basin area so steamy back at the Tiki Barn, and glared without subtlety at me.

I had perhaps steamed things up just a bit.

I had considered, given my knowledge of properties and gasses and elementals of all natures, that very hot water might scrape off the small scattering of spots that had resolutely refused to take their leave of my hairline and which I was beginning to think were in fact freckles, which would be cause for much celebration, were it true, but in whose truth I dared not let myself believe until I had exhausted every means of evacuation in my arsenal.

It was quite a tantrum The Lamb had, before setting off to the place.

The rest of us followed under separate cover; we were not after all stars of stage-acting.

The protest outside the venue had not let up for a moment it would seem since our run-in with the born-agains. They were, if anything, stronger in number and heartier of spirit, with the introduction of shrimps and Tiki Ty's dipping into their diet. Their cholesterol had gone down. Their energy level had gone up. They let us move unmolested through their protest into the theater, falling out as though gods passed, though they were holding many other audience members up.

We could hear them, our fellow ticket-holders, protesting the protestors throughout the performance.

Their faraway shouts did nothing to diminish the play's success.

Perhaps it had been misleading, earlier, to label The Lamb's play a disappointment?

This perhaps had the unintended consequence of indicating that the play did not go off so well?

The play went off splendidly.

I, I must admit, wept.

I wept and laughed and gripped Murphy's arm to my left and Binelli's arm to my right and cheered and booed and leapt to my feet at the curtain's close to woo the stage-actors back out before us to bask in the glory they'd created.

That the play was after all such an overwhelming success, that The Lamb's performance in particular was written up with lavish praise in all the columns, *this* was the disappointment to which I referred.

A personal disappointment that has no place in an objective account.

# 63

—**Do you remember,** said Murphy, —the Great China Wall?

—Do you remember, I said, —how it's not called that.

Murphy jangled his pockets. The day outside the warm wood of the Tiki Barn was as was its wont quite gray, and heavy, heavy with quiet.

—Do you remember, said Murphy, —a time when you were not so difficult all the time?

—I do not, I said, —remember such a time.

I tried to remember the time at the Great China Wall and then remembered how I was remembering the name wrong myself now that Murphy had remembered it wrong, and I remembered how I suggested to Murphy to remember how it wasn't called that and then how Murphy asked me to remember a time when I was not so difficult and how I did not.

—Do you, I said.

—Do I what, said Murphy.

Jangle, jangle.

—Remember.

—Remember what, said Murphy.

—A time when I was not so difficult.

The jangling stopped but Murphy didn't fill its absence with anything like words.

—Or a time when you didn't jangle your pockets so, I said. I could sometimes be useful. Sometimes one remembering can lead to another. —For instance, I said, —did you jangle so at the Great China Wall.

—Do you remember me jangling?

I thought back. At the Great China Wall had been a scene of terrific disarray.

—I perhaps remember a tambourine? I said.

I remembered perhaps not a tambourine. It had been a great and terrible disarray, back at the Great China Wall, with noise-making coming from every direction. We had done not so much harm, but we had done some, there.

—I remember Binelli getting a little something wrong about the Great China Wall, I said. —And it leading to a fantastic disarray.

Murphy jangled agreeably. He was remembering too, and it gave him a small delight.

How wrong Binelli had been. How rarely had ever Binelli been so wrong.

Binelli had gone in fact quite apoplectic. The remembering knotted my very loins.

I remembered setting my satchel with heavy Lavendar upon a large slab of the Great China Wall and how agitated the extremely lazy and asleep Lavendar became. I thought the slab was hot perhaps but although the sun was shining down upon the Great China Wall it was not after all hot to the touch. Lavendar came quite out of his satchel, which he could and can whenever he chooses and chose then to do, though mostly he doesn't because of his extreme propensity toward languor. He tossed me a black look from atop the Great China Wall and waited, and I picked up the satchel from that great slab of Great China Wall and set it open and attractively upon the ground and Lavendar got right back inside and fell right back to sleep.

As far as I know, he fell right back to sleep.

—I thought you remembered everything so well, said Murphy. —With excruciating attention to detail.

—What were we remembering, exactly, I said.

—If I jangled.

—I perhaps exaggerated my attention to detail, then, I said, —in that case.

—I have jangled for as long as you can remember, Murphy said.

Which was, I thought, an odd way of putting things, but odd is mostly Murphy's way. And has been for as long as I can remember.

# 64

Binelli burst out the front of the Tiki Barn and into our midst.

—Finley, he said.

—Binelli, I said.

—Murphy, Binelli said.

—Binelli, Murphy said.

—Murphy, Binelli said. —You may take your leave.

Murphy took his leave.

Binelli glared and waved his hands a bit. —What have I said about remembering the alleged snafu at the Great China Wall.

—That what I remember about the Great China Wall has been traditionally not quite exactly right, I admitted.

I was mired in regret.

How had he heard us.

Binelli was mired in fury.

—Do you know, Binelli said, —what day this is?

I did not.

Had I known, I likely would still have remained silent, so mired in fury was Binelli.

—It is, Binelli said, quaking, —the anniversary of Sacco and Vanzetti.

—Mmmm, I said. I would admit to nothing.

We arrived at a stalling point in the conversation.

Binelli shook and in all likelihood glared upon me with a dark and penetrating glare.

I, giving the ground the same dark and penetrating glare, could not for absolutely certain see Binelli's glare, but one could assume quite safely even if one were not ordinarily given to assumptions that it was impressive.

The ground, more heroic and stalwart than I, gazed impassively back at me rather than casting its own glare askance at another, weaker entity; the ground deserved credit for nipping in the bud then a sort of Russian-doll effect with the glares.

I gave the ground its due.

Its small due.

If it had wanted to look away, I'm not convinced it could have.

—Finley, said Binelli.

—Binelli, I said.

—Is there a Tension between us.

I met his dark and penetrating glare.

I grasped the air a bit, seeking—what—a spray bottle.

Or was it even required.

I did an experiment. I leaned almost imperceptibly closer to Binelli's great and fearsome head.

Binelli did not flinch away.

And me dry as ice.

—I think we both know there is, I said.

Not as ice. As sand.

Desert sand, rather than beach sand.

I leaned in, perceptibly now, closer.

For beach sand does tend toward the damp.

—I know *I* know, Binelli said.

With that, a torrid and untranslatable interlude passed.

# 65

**Or, for the sake of accuracy,** Binelli leaned aft, perceptibly, and wondered aloud several things.

—Know there is what, was one thing he wondered.

—Why are you lunging at me, was another.

—Do you not sweat, was a third. —You're dryer than naked
bones.

# 66

**The opening of Rogan's gallery show** came soon after The Lamb's triumphant opening; what a dizzying life we led. I should say the public opening of Rogan's show. Rogan's show opened to the public about a week after Rogan's show first opened to some select viewers—of whom we were conspicuously, mind you, not some—who were necessary not only to view but to participate in the show.

To create the show, as it were.

For without that week of pre-viewers, to which, mind you, we were rather rudely to my thinking not invited, there would have been in fact nothing at all to show.

Being that the viewers took the pictures.

Nevertheless, the opening to the public, that ungainly horde of which we made up a tidy clump, was a lavish affair. There's a chicken-and-egg conundrum in red velvet ropes: Are the ropes necessary because of the ungainly horde expected to come, or does the ungainly horde come because it sees red velvet ropes. Either way, there were red velvet ropes and an ungainly horde each, straining against one another furiously, trying to keep out and get in, respectively.

We were egregiously underdressed.

I was egregiously underdressed. Would be the more accurate statement.

High heels tottered through the gravel, bringing lady after lady to her knees. My heels were not high but rather a sensible blend of the best Japanese samurai and Roman gladiator innovations had to offer. I could crunch quite mannishly across any length of gravel without twisting a twittering ankle or finding myself splayed skirt akimbo someplace up around the torsic region, if a skirt I'd worn, which I had not, another misstep, never mind. I strode mannishly without a shred of shame over broken bits of chiffon-clad shoulders and helpless diamonded pinkie fingers and stepped my hard Japanese footbeds over shimmering chignons toward the rope.

The Lamb looked up at me with pleading eyes. Her smuggled size 9.5 stilettos had been her ruin. Still smarting over her recent success on the stage, I did not reach out my hand to her.

Nor did I, however, kick gravel into her face.

I strode with purpose through the clamoring crowd, right up to the front of the line, where unsurprisingly I gained swift untroubled entrance to the gallery, looking so much for all intents and purposes like a critic of some sort, perhaps, or a madwoman from France. For who else would be garbed so. Who else could possibly command such footwear. Who, the doorkeepers must have considered in that split second of thought between seeing and granting me passage into the coveted lair, would even have been invited to such a fashionable affair with so little fashion sense if not someone so unfashionable they were somehow beyond fashion and therefore in fact at the very throbbing center of it.

This last perhaps a stretch but then again perhaps not.

The interior was stark but for all the glittering crowd. The walls were a simple white, the moldings a simple blond wood, the floors simply belonging in a barn. Rogan would mention in interviews after the fact in a strangling high-pitched tone of hysteria that there was nothing whatsoever simple in the specific shade of white he'd chosen, and mixed himself for accuracy, and had applied to the walls in evenly timed coats until every undertone of the previous, lamentable white had been eradicated and could no longer cast its naive, almost insulting, pallor upon his palette.

Be that as it may.

In the center of the room was Rogan. He sat on a simple wooden stool, unaware for all the world of the crowd swarming him and his toney white walls, working at a piece of driftwood. He was dressed simply in a simple white shirt and simple denim trousers and simple leather sandals, looking ever the picture of simple hardworking simplicity, simple on a stool as I'd tell him later and for which comment he would practically wring my neck before remembering the touchy snakes in the room and backing off.

Directly in front of Rogan but several feet away stood a camera on a tripod. It was trained upon Rogan. This was where the art of the artwork was to occur.

How Rogan's show worked was this: The crowd would take pictures, as they saw fit, of Rogan himself, at work on his frames. They would take all the pictures in the world, all in classy black and white, of him in his various moods, fresh-faced in the morning and shadowed by a slow-to-arrive five o'clock. They would photograph him as he tied his hair back in his dusty blue bandanna, as he sucked a finger sliced by hanging wire, as he surveyed with dispassion the filling walls around him. Mostly they would photograph him as he simply worked, making frame after frame for the pictures they took, blandly crafting his wares as the crowds ebbed and flowed around him, for the crowds too, perusing the framed prints on the walls, would be captured as background matter and become the exhibit.

The film was developed as rolls reached their limits by a crack team of art interns, all so very grateful and awestruck to find themselves part of this blockbuster project that they barely spoke, barely smiled, barely paused to eat or sleep or notice the absence of a daily paycheck or food allowance. They unloaded the camera reverently, as though each picture weren't expendable, as though each precious roll contained the final frames of a photographic legend before his expiration by emphysema. They would bring the developed photographs back in simple black boxes, and lay them like reverent Magi at Rogan's feet. He acknowledged neither their comings nor goings, just acted as though the boxes had been there all along and dutifully continued making frames for the pictures within.

The show's nature guaranteed return patronage. Whose plunging backline, whose tossed strands of hair would be caught behind Rogan? Whose picture would be deemed worthy of wall space? Whose would be ignored, unframed, left to gather dust and be trampled underfoot? Some patrons would make sport of attempting to take a photo of Rogan framing their earlier-snapped photo, working themselves into uncomfortable lathers and remaining in the gallery from sun-up to -down, all toward that triumphant moment when they would cease playing pawn in this artgame and become instead master. Indeed, the swanky cognoscenti and those aspiring to join its ranks would become positively rabid about the show, returning day after day, in the hopes of writing their own starring role into its script.

Some interns—those art students presumably who lacked talent—served hors d'oeuvres on thin wooden trays, whose most astonishing feature was an absence of shrimps.

I plucked toothpicks from the trays with severe bad temper. Fishes, yes, and meats and cheeses, and that most awkward of fruit, the fig, appeared, but not a shrimp in the whole production.

Rogan was gunning for me, of this I became certain.

I chewed a sad fig. They were not enjoying a great popularity among the crowd. I helped where I could. I washed it down with fizzy water and took another from the next eye-height tray that passed.

The Lamb was a bit bedraggled from her spill outside but she knew as did everyone with eyes that her bedragglement and tiny knee-spots of blood granted her acceptance among the crowd that I would never receive, misperceptions as to my station notwithstanding, so she deigned to stand with me and watch the proceedings.

We fended off several gentlemen well past their expiration dates who found her charms irresistible.

I fended off several gentlemen well past their expiration dates who found her charms irresistible would be a more accurate account of the fending. The Lamb looked demurely at her too-big shoes and bit her bottom lip and barely threw an elbow.

Binelli moved into the invisible sacred circle that sealed off Rogan from the rest of us and the crowd murmured its scandalized objection.

Binelli paid them no mind.

An opportunistic top-hatted fop rushed in to capture the invasion on film.

Binelli said a few words out of the corner of his mouth to Rogan, who continued to frame away as he answered. Binelli tapped at his watch pointedly; Rogan gestured at the crowd with his head. They conducted a remarkably long conversation this way, Binelli leering and nagging at Rogan and the *artiste* with amazing dexterity not missing a beat in his work.

They arrived at some conclusion and Binelli moved away.

A tremendously tall lady tried to make her way to the stool but some interns strong-armed her back to the ring's periphery.

What business did Binelli have with Rogan it occurred to me to wonder.

Had Binelli co-opted my Assignment. Was he Investigating on the side, Investigating perhaps me. Investigating my Investigation. Had Rogan been somehow on the inside of our operation all along—an embedded spy, suffering Odille's obscene affections in order to, once we'd arrived, win my trust.

And how had Kiki B gained admission to the pre-view week.

For I noticed all at once that one of the photographs, already framed and hanging low on the not-simply-white wall directly across from me, included her, in the background, turning to face the camera at the moment of the flash.

Did Rogan know everyone.

I moved closer to the photograph and as I did I got an electric feeling that I couldn't quite put my finger on. It felt in a way like Lavendar's skin, but on the inside. Kiki B's head in the photograph was at the level of my own, our eyes meeting straight on, her gaze unsurprised at the camera's flash. A tipsy couple careened between us, clinking glasses and laughing showily, and once they'd passed I realized what the strangeness was: In black and white, Kiki B looked just like me.

It was as though I'd caught my reflection in the window of a darkened storefront. In reflections, one's for example horrid red hair has no color, only degrees of light and shadow. In reflections, one's horrid yellow eyes appear nothing more than vague drops of gray in white pools. One's skin is not freckled, or not not freckled; only the bones and barest facts remain.

My and Kiki B's barest facts were identical.

# 67

**Binelli swept up** beside me in his zaftig way.

—We have to go, he said. —We've done our bit. This is about to wind down anyhow.

I pointed toward the photograph. —Is it, I said, —my imagination, or does—

—Murphy is already waiting outside, Binelli said, reorienting my entire posture in the direction of the gallery entrance as though I were a toddler just learning to walk. —As is Tiki Ty. If I can now only wrest That Lamb from the elderly clutches of this esteemed art community, which wants lessons in propriety and perversity I must say, he gestured to the corner where The Lamb was indeed acting the rope in a geriatric sort of tug-of-war, —we can be on our way, having donated a not-ungenerous portion of our evening to the arts and cultures, et cetera.

He paused with almost a wondering face. —I did think this stage would pass once the performance had done. You don't suppose. He shook his head. —The role will wear off in time. Which we do not currently have in luxurious droves. Let us take our leave.

He clapped his hands once, sharply, and I moved toward the door, propelled after a spell by his gentle little warning push.

Murphy and Tiki Ty were waiting just outside the doorway fray.

The clamor both within and without the velvet ropes had not died down whatsoever. Women were baring their eager breasts. Men were flashing wads of currency and loosening their ties. Reputations were on the line and lines were being carved with angry pointed toes into the gravel.

Murphy and Tiki Ty incidentally were both appropriately dressed for the opening.

Tiki Ty looked positively Cuban in a linen variation on his scrubbish flowing garb, coral-hued, and topped with a straw fedora. Murphy was dapper in another way altogether, in a slim dust-gray three-piece suit.

Had there been a memorandum I'd missed.

Tiki Ty and Murphy were smoking cigars and having a mildly amused conversation between puffs as to the nature of genius and crowds and power and commerce and art and culture and so forth. I interrupted on what I could tell Murphy thought a really salient point and he stared reproachfully at me as I redirected Tiki Ty's attention.

Is Kiki B, I said, at all Russian.

—She wouldn't appear to be, said Tiki Ty, less aggrieved than Murphy with my interruption, having not been evidently as impassioned a player in their debating game. —Though I suppose the Russians as do we all vary greatly in their collective aspect. Their countenance. Their *visage*, if you will. Making absolute identification as such difficult if not outright impossible.

He paused for a long puff of his cigar.

I turned then to Murphy, but Tiki Ty had not done.

—You, Tiki Ty said, —for instance, do not to my general recognitive powers as such resemble so very much a Russian. With the bare shabby tools I own, no, your eyes for instance are not set so deep in your skull, for one.

What had that to do with anything I had no idea and I addressed Murphy over Tiki Ty's continuing smoke-spewing ramble.

—Am I quite like Kiki B, I said. —That you've had occasion to notice.

—You are nothing, Murphy said firmly, —like Kiki B.

He then chewed his cigar thoughtfully.

When he was ready to continue, he spoke very carefully. —Kiki B is everything you are not.

Before I had time even to begin an indignant bristling phase, Murphy said quickly, —And vice versa. There is no single aspect you and Kiki B share. It is as though, Murphy said, —there was one pot of goods, which was split evenly down the middle, half allotted to Kiki B and half allotted to you. If you were to combine, he stared at me with uncomfortable unblinkingness as he said this last bit, —if you were to *combine*, in fact, you would become—

Binelli burst through the crowd with The half-dressed Lamb in tow. He was buttoning her blouse and mumbling as if to himself and himself alone, —It's like keeping a monkey-house.

Once The Lamb had regained the small modicum of decency she possessed, Binelli took charge of us all with a cold appraising gaze. —We'll be quite late, he said. —We'll have to take a cart. Two carts. We'll roll there in a barrel, how about. Won't we be a spectacle.

Binelli was quite furious and discomfited. It was rare to see him in a fluster and we all I can safely report were equal parts entertained and nervous. All equal parts but for myself, I considered, working back up the indignant bristling that Murphy had earlier cut off before it had reached its great bristling prime. But for myself, who was only half parts anything. Quite then incomplete. A ragtag arm here, a couple of toes, a nostril without nose, an earlobe attached to a high Russian forehead.

We piled into a single golfing cart though we were too many, far too many. Binelli barked out steering instructions to a beleaguered Tiki Ty, who had a squirming Murphy half in his lap and a glowering cigar in his mouth and several of my parts in several of his places.

I couldn't, you see, help it, my silent bristling invective continued as we careened loudly across the gravel at dangerous speed,

. being so *half*. Being such an incomplete scrap heap of limb and mind. One can hardly be expected can one to control—

Why was my invective toward Murphy always cut off.

We screeched to a halt.

# 68

—At last, Binelli said. —It all comes to this.

I thought that was possibly overreaching. The *this* to which he gestured with such grandiosity was nothing but a bowling emporium, from whose doors we'd parked at a slight askew distance.

It was, granted, the most tremendous bowling emporium I had ever seen. Its enormity was of a scope to be reckoned with. It was goggling.

Binelli was if I was not mistaken trembling.

It was mind-boggling. Boggling to the mind. Not goggling. Though if one considered, logically, it was goggling as well, at least about the eyes.

In that one's eyes bulged from the sheer mind-boggling enormity of the emporium, creating the impression that one was, for all intents and purposes, wearing goggles.

It was as though he were nervous.

—We'll be wanting, Binelli said, —to secure the perimeter. He tucked and gestured at us. He darted and swiveled about the eyes and neck. —I'll just nip my head in. Scope it out.

He was definitely trembling.

—Keep to the shadows, Binelli said. —Yet close at hand.

He positioned us like chess pieces and gave a single hand clap, lacking it must be noted authority, before dashing inside.

Murphy pulled me out of my vague positioning. He used his low tones. —Is it my imagination or is Binelli, he said, —nervous?

—Nowhere in my imagination, I said somewhat imperiously, —exists any prior image of Binelli being nervous to which I can compare the present Binelli. But the nature of imagination, I suppose, I said, —is that it comes up with these wild new things all the time?

—But about this, Murphy said. —Finley, he said. —I'm not imagining?

—Will you wait, I said.

I felt a bit goggled. There was strange information hovering in the air around my head like so many mosquitoes, biting not often but at random intervals in unexpected places. I was having some trouble I admit, though to admit is something I am loathe to do, adjusting to the new circumstances.

I took my leave. Of my station, of Murphy, the lot.

I stood alone at the great glass doors of the bowling emporium, hoarding air. I looked all around at the nothing but gravel. It stretched far as any eye could see. It was a gravel river graveling its gray way through warehouse banks, reeds of rusted chain-link, the sky just sky but gray as gravel and of equally little use.

Then something.

There were strained sounds of some strange music, carried by a wind I could not account for. In that there was no wind I could account for. But still, the music, carried somehow through perfectly still air.

I followed the sound coming from no direction in what turned out to be the right direction, in that its source was soon revealed. It was coming from behind more great glass doors, just like the doors of the bowling emporium except a bit farther along the gravel and these great glass doors being painted quite opaque with blackening. One would not expect such music to be behind them, for now the music was not in the slightest strained, and the doors seemed of not enough consequence to contain a music so robust.

So swanky.

I pushed very slightly on one of the doors.

It was not locked.

I proceeded with a little bit of caution, but such caution proved difficult to maintain in the face of such swanky music. My caution was infiltrated by a whiff of shimmy. My caution was compromised by a snifter of sidestep. My caution collapsed into cocksure *caliente*. My caution fell finally away into a frenzied frug.

The people inside took no notice of my frug's flawlessness, a flawless frug just par for the course in a joint like this. I took a partner and we took care of business. We mashed the potato. We did the twist. We popped the corn and hankied the panky and we walked the dog until the dog planted his back legs as best he could on such a polished wood floor and refused to go any farther.

My nameless partner and I separated with empty promises and tearful graspings, and I limped to the refreshment stand to punch myself sated for the next round.

Punch, the red beverage. Not punch, the fists of fury. Punching myself with the fists of fury would have had the opposite effect than that intended. Punching myself would have made further dancing impossible, and my objective with the punch—the red beverage punch—was to make further dancing not only possible but unstoppable.

I drank one punch quickly and then ladled another to sip over time.

I knew how to take a punch.

Murphy surprised me at the punch table. He was already drinking his punch, presumably his second, judging by his already-refreshed aspect. Had he followed me. Had he been dancing. Had so much time passed. I hadn't done much noticing, during. Once in the dance I do have a tendency to lose my edge in powers of observation. I am told that my eyes spend much of their free time while the rest of me is dancing rolling epileptically back in my head. I am told that it's actually somewhat of an improvement to my general mien, in that my eyes are less frightening when only the whites are available for viewing and the rest can be imagined as quite nice eyes, hazel perhaps, or the color of a new tortoise.

Murphy tipped the rim of his paper cup toward me in greeting. —This is some place, he said, yelling a bit to be heard over the music, which had taken no notice of my absence from the dance floor and swanked on without me, lost in its own reveries. —I'd wondered what it was when I saw it from above. There's a big . . . No, *guess*. Guess what's painted on the roof of this place.

—On the roof, I repeated, distracted. Then, tracking back, —From above?

—A flamingo! Murphy almost clapped with glee. Except he was holding of course the cup. He splashed with glee punch across his lapel. —A flamingo!

—What are you doing here, I said.

—We're all here, he said. He gestured toward the dance floor where, mingled in among the dapper dancers were The Lamb and Tiki Ty. They were flimflamming all over the place.

O, the hair on them. So black, so much. They could outfit an army of follicle-challenged charlatans, setting sales of hair tonic through the roof. At least Tiki Ty's was up out of the way. The Lamb with a long sweaty streak plastered across her face looked mustachioed.

Yet somehow dignified, I must admit.

The band played a filthy series of notes, and simultaneously Murphy and I drained and flung aside our paper cups and returned to the dance floor. It was serious. The floor cleared but for me and Murphy, and The Lamb and Tiki Ty. We moved in a remarkable almost preordained unison Binelli would have appreciated to the four corners of a square only there once we'd arrived.

Our timing was perfect, or the band's was. They hit their blue note as we hit our marks, and we all paused.

The crowd nearly passed out.

It began.

We all knew the steps and the direction in which to take them. We knew the sharp turns, the slow dips, the half-downs. The band played a honeyed golden wheatfield draped in muddied pinafores. A deep sliding string took a turn in the hay with a ragged horn and prim pianola. The grass stains were beyond washing, the very dirt beneath the scene of the tryst ruined forever to planting and tidy rows.

It went on for a very long while.

Murphy was across from me and we moved like images in a half-cracked mirror, always opposite, fun-house style. He knew my every whim, matched me improvisation for improvisation. In the corners I liked to give an extra kick, broken-horse bent at an odd angle from the knee, and even this he echoed, even the attached head and wrist flicks.

When had we danced before.

Certainly not here. This dance hall was ancient, but new to us. A similar dance hall certainly was somewhere in existence but not in my memory. And I so like a pachyderm since the silence remained yet fishy about the beforetime.

Though a dance is an unlocking thing.

**Battersea beckoned,** from just outside the dance hall's edges, a gesture I could not let pass unanswered. An open door, a hardwood floor . . . I was perhaps in need of a rest, perhaps madeleines.

# 70

**But first, I had to finish** the Quadrille.

The dance, properly executed, has neither beginning nor end. One enters the dance as though relaxing back into one's own breathing, after a momentary and dangerous hiatus, and does not, to make the metaphor really do its proper job, stop breathing again lightly.

One dancer leaving makes the whole thing collapse in on itself. A triangle cannot Quadrille. Ideally, the decision to end the Quadrille should be a delicate dance of its own. It should last at least as long as the dancing lasts. There should pass many passes between participants of searching eye, hidden glance, et cetera. There should be slowings and quickenings, as if testing the possibility of closing the Quadrille. These tests should be tentative and subtle and ultimately futile.

It can take a terribly long time to attempt an end to the Quadrille.

It wasn't really time I had.

I stepped out and the Quadrille collapsed horribly. The entire dance hall gasped. They advanced upon me as one extremely livid yet dapper body.

No one appreciates a premature finish.

Murphy stepped between the crowd and me and held up a commanding hand. —She has business, he said. —There's corruption afoot. She paused for a Quadrille in ritzy digs, but it would be irresponsible if she ignored now the matter at hand. Let it be, he said.

The crowd dropped their weapons, which were their hands, which held punch cups, which spilled punch all over the smartly polished dance hall floor. It looked, of course, as though violent ends had been met. They would perhaps let the next stranger worry over it. But they would let me go, wishing me silent yet undeniably *swanky* godspeed.

I took my leave.

# 71

**Murphy found me** collecting myself, which was taking longer as a process than my abrupt exit would have otherwise indicated, outside the imposing blackened glass doorway. He was followed shortly thereafter by the disgruntled other members of the Quadrille. The Lamb shoved me very hard and then acted as though she hadn't. She acted it so well I let it pass, wondering almost if it was all in my head. Tiki Ty just leaned against the wall in a post-Quadrille slump. A Quadrille is hard to kick. I felt as much guilt as my wiring allowed.

—You missed all the action, Murphy said.

—Did they all slip in the punch, I said. I pictured all that finery, sopping and punched up. I pictured the ire rising for a second time, and wondered whether we might just be wise to step away from the building.

—They would never slip in the punch, Tiki Ty said with terrific depression. —They are far too dignified.

—They would never just drop the Quadrille, either, The Lamb said. —They are far too classy.

—I'm sorry I dropped the Quadrille, I said. I meant it too. —But I got a feeling.

—Back at the lanes, Murphy said, —I meant.

—Are you still talking, The Lamb said. She was very ill-tempered now. She too was up against the Quadrille hangover. I'd get it as well, in time. I had at the moment the adrenaline against it, but there's no staving it off forever.

—Back at the bowling emporium, Murphy said, —I meant. The action at the bowling emporium.

—What action, I said. —Binelli bowled. Binelli always bowls.

—*We* bowled, Murphy said.

—Binelli would never let you bowl, I said.

Never is a minor misstatement. Binelli had let us bowl, once. We had not been impressive bowlers, not as a group nor as individuals. Binelli had raged and chased us around with bowling pins, and tore up all the scorecards, and berated us with insults. He'd subsequently bowled alone rather than suffer ever again the humiliation, and possibly contagion, of bowling with those for whom bowling is not even an accurate term.

For what we did.

When we tried to bowl.

Which had been just the once.

—O we bowled all right, said The Lamb. —I bowled, Murphy bowled. Tiki Ty bowled.

She gave a long dramatic pause. —You bowled, The Lamb said.

Everyone looked at me expectantly.

—I did not bowl, I said.

The bowling had been I think the worst for me, the time we bowled. I'd of course had no recollection of previous bowling, so the entire endeavor had been particularly farcical when my turn came up. No bodily sense memory arose within me, steering me absent my mind toward the proper motions. I perhaps had actually never encountered bowling, even before the silence. It certainly didn't ring any bells during the ill-fated bowling, and I was hurt doing the bowling in fact, quite injured, about the fingers and toes, and in the wrist and forearm, and in the shin a bit, and then a little bit on my head.

—But you did, Murphy said. —We all did. We all bowled our hearts out.

227

—We're likely bowling still, said Tiki Ty.

The punch had gotten to them.

—The punch has gotten to you, I said. —Go back. Find a fourth for a Quadrille until its effects wear off. I have business to which I must attend.

—It's not the punch, Murphy said. —Come see.

—What business, he said.

—I have to go to Battersea, I said.

—It can wait, Murphy said. —It can. You should come.

I let my knees buckle and my eyes roll up just slightly as we started back the long lonely gravel road to the bowling emporium, so they would note my vast and profound displeasure, but I went all the same. Antipathy loves company and all that. And my Quadrille aftereffects were starting to hit. Murphy and Tiki Ty, at least, could prove useful in the case my body needed propping. Up or otherwise.

# 72

**The first thing I noticed** upon entering the bowling emporium was Lavendar's head poking out of his satchel like a prairie dog's.

He looked immeasurably concerned.

I couldn't believe I'd left him. And not noticed for all that time. I rushed over to him, poor Lavendar, so unceremoniously positioned among so many unfamiliar satchels upon a littered snack-bar table. His eyes darted from me to the center lane, quickly, and back again. His look was an utter daze—a new look for Lavendar, who veers between cold calculation and beady sizing-up, and sometimes, toward me, just a touch of the louche barfly.

I followed his eyes on their next trip, laneward.

I was there, in the center lane, bowling.

**73**

I was unexpectedly proficient.

# 74

I brought the ball to my chin as I'd seen Binelli do, ball-less, a thousand times in Tiki Ty's various sitting rooms. I paused, took a visible breath, tossed my high ponytail imperiously, and hurled the ball down the lane.

I knocked all the pins down in a thunderclap.

Binelli, Tiki Ty, Murphy, and The Lamb raised their fists and cheered.

We were all dressed in splendid team uniforms, cobalt blue with bold black piping. We all wore matching black bowling shoes with nonslip soles.

Clearly not rentals, a fact within which I took quick solace.

We were all over there in that coveted center lane, surrounded by one-gloved art interns, bowling the match of our life. And we were all, save Binelli, simultaneously back in the snack bar, watching our impressive performance from a distance.

We'd been twinned.

I stared about me.

Murphy nodded. —You see.

—I told you, The Lamb said triumphantly, —that you bowled.

Tiki Ty shook his head. —I'm not supposed to be part of this, really, he said. —I'm not really even *of* you guys.

He stared off at his double. —I mean, I would never wear that outfit. I kind of wish he'd left me out of it.

—I guess the team required five, Murphy said.

—But who are they, I said.

—Isn't that your area of expertise, said The Lamb. —Aren't you the one Assigned to Puppets?

A little bit became clear.

Then, as I considered, a little bit more.

—Puppets, I said. —I see.

I didn't see clearly, but I saw just enough of a crumby trail through the fog that I could take a few first tentative steps. Was I sure they were quite small, Binelli had said. Was I sure they weren't in fact bigger.

Lavendar tentatively struck at my hand with his tiny forked tongue. I petted his head. I rubbed my index finger between his eyes like he liked.

And everyone bowling was a bit, I tried to remember how Odille had put it, jerky. In their way.

—So Mr. Uppal, Murphy began.

I cut him off automatically. —Professor.

—So Professor Uppal, Murphy said dourly, —was in on it with Binelli.

I shook my head. That didn't seem right. I'd asked after larger Puppets. The Professor had been quite adamant. No bigger, he'd said. No need for that. Rogan, he'd said, had asked him the same thing and why did the later generations always want everything bigger all the time?

I'm framing the Professor, Rogan had said.

Rogan's the only one interested in Daddy's toys, Odille had said.

Which way had Odille gone to meet Rogan, Binelli had said.

I sat down upon a snack-bar barstool, my post-Quadrille hang-over meeting politely and with a wan handshake my realization that I was possibly the very worst Investigator of the group.

Rogan appeared before me, emanating light.

—You should really try to stay out of sight, he said. —It might cause confusion, having you both here.

—It might cause confusion, I said.

What Assignment could I possibly draw after this.

—You know, Rogan said, his tone holding no hint of apology nor explanation and expanding as he spoke to include the whole group, —both sets.

Rogan looked in fact quite proud. —They're pretty good, right, he said, surveying our champion bowling twins in the center lane. —I mean, down to the last detail. It was tricky you know, he said, —getting it all right. I didn't spend much time with some of you. I had to work from description, mostly, and photographs. Good thing Binelli keeps such extensive files.

Center lane Tiki Ty rolled for a spare.

Snack-bar Tiki Ty looked slightly ashamed.

—Why do I seem like a lesser bowler, he said to Rogan.

—Well someone had to be second-string, Rogan said. —I mean, it would just look odd, you know. Everyone rolling nothing, he said, —but strikes. He dropped his voice confidentially. —And you know, you're not really as much *of* them, if you catch my drift. I mean, from what Binelli says, you're always pretty much there, anyhow, but officially. I mean, you're more of an independent, right.

This explanation seemed to satisfy Tiki Ty. He smoothed some wrinkles from his cool linen trousers and wondered if anyone would very much object to his finishing off his cigar.

No one objected very much, although The Lamb objected just a bit, until The Lamb in the center lane struck a dagger through the lane's very heart. Pins scattered impressive distances. The Lamb in the snack bar raised her fists triumphantly then, and wondered if she might have a celebratory cigar of her own. —A victory cigar, she said. —I'm doing so well, aren't I. I look quite the part in that uniform, don't you think. Cobalt blue, she said, —flatters me tremendously. I'm sure Binelli chose it for exactly that reason, don't you suspect.

—Well, Rogan said, —there really was just kind of a lot of co-balt fabric in the—

Odille appeared next to Rogan and hit him several times about the head and shoulders and a little bit in the tender midsection area, halting what would have been a bit of satisfactory dressing-down of The Lamb.

Satisfactory to myself, that is.

Quite unsatisfactory to The Lamb.

Probably neutral to the others.

Maybe just a bit satisfactory to the others.

—You did this, Odille said to Rogan. —You had them Investigating my father. You had me thinking my mother was going to pasture.

—Did I not *say,* Rogan said, looking at me for confirmation, —right out loud and in the open that I was framing Odille's father? Didn't I say that?

—He did, I said, remembering that first meeting in the café.

He had pulled out an actual frame at the time, which could be construed as misleading, to be sure, but there was no getting around that ancient admission.

—I've never been anything but honest, Rogan said. —I said I was working on something. I met with your father right in front of you. I always showed an interest in the Puppets. I would've brought him in on it if he'd wanted. He didn't want, Rogan said, —bigger Puppets. He wanted no part of it. But if he had—

Binelli stalked up on us, looking slightly taxed though trium-phant around the edges. —Do you suppose, he said tersely, —that you could keep it down over here. It's very distracting. And poten-tially confusing for the audience.

Binelli wore a glove too, just like the Professor's. Just like the interns.

—It's just she's being so accusatory, Rogan said, casting a hurt look toward Odille.

I almost stroked his cheek, so hurt was his look, a poor dull glimmer, but I refrained, seeing as he had so masterfully and willfully and deceitfully twinned us. It would take some time and many tender coercive blandishments on his part before I would stroke his cheek. I held my stroking hand firmly to my side.

—Why accusing, Binelli said, looking over at Odille. His gaze which had begun in so casual a manner intensified upon her. —Who is this, he said. He didn't take his eyes off her, and when no one answered he gestured wildly and repeated, —Who?!

—Odille, I said. —The Professor's daughter. I told you about her.

—How obese she is. The Lamb giggled, ignoring Odille's clear and present lack of obesity in favor of the delightful taste of the misspeak. —How grotesquely obese.

Odille met and matched the intensity of Binelli's gaze. —And you, she said, —must be the Puppet Master.

Did Binelli *blush* or had the lighting merely shifted, lowered, reddened and warmed.

—Well Rogan did all the—

—Rogan was a pawn, Odille said. —But you, she said. —You pulled the strings.

Binelli's coloring deepened further, or the light further shifted, lowered, et cetera.

Either way.

He looked toward the ground. And then something broke open on his face. —Your feet, he said, staring at Odille's feet.

—I know, she said. —They're huge.

—Obese, said The Lamb encouragingly.

—Wait, Murphy said. —This whole Investigation was to win at *bowling*?

—What size, Binelli said, but I could tell he already knew.

—9.5, Odille said, years of apology in her voice.

—Is no one, Murphy said, —at all *offended*? Is this not the most *malevolent,* I mean, even more so than usual—

—Would you, Binelli said, almost in a whisper, —accept these.

He delicately removed the single glove from his right hand. He dug around through the mound of satchels on the snack-bar table until he found his own. He pulled from his satchel a pristine brown box. He pulled from this box a pair of shoes, bowling shoes, but like no bowling shoes you've ever seen. The softest hide, the color and texture of fresh butter. Stitching almost otherworldly in its tiny tidy perfection. Soled as if soleless, soles one could pad through miles of gravel with and not make a sound, and not feel a pebble, and not disturb a dung beetle.

—I mean, come *on,* Murphy said. —I went up in a blimp. A blimp! I risked my *life.*

Odille held out her hands reverently. She ran her lovely fingers along the lovely leather, making small sounds of appreciation at each new wonder she discovered. She kicked out of her own bulky gravel-crunchers and slipped her long toes into Binelli's gift.

The shoe was made for her foot and vice versa. She held up the perfection at the end of her leg for all to admire. She turned it this way and that so as not to exclude any portion of flawlessness from our collective view. She took her own eyes off this foot long enough to gaze at Binelli, and he felt her gaze and met it.

Rogan protested heedlessly.

—You want to get out of here, Murphy said to me.

I'd forgotten in all the excitement about Kiki B and Battersea.

—I do, I said.

We took our leave, snatching up Lavendar, who felt heavier than usual, likely with depression, and no one seemed to notice our exit. The shoes had intoxicated them. And there were more of us there in any case, in case we were missed, and they far better bowlers than we besides.

# 75

We took a cart to Battersea.

We made almost no small talk along the way. There had been so much activity. It was fine to crunch through the great gravel roads and notice only small tournaments and festivals and demonstrations every so often to our right or left.

—You drive the cart admirably, Murphy did say at one juncture.

At another: —I don't think The Lamb's performance was *that* brilliant.

I thanked him both times. They were generous gestures. I felt fondly toward Murphy, and he hardly jangled his pockets at all though the ride was long and much had happened.

Battersea's gray ladies welcomed us, and let us go on our own toward Kiki B's bungalow. They were having, they explained, a fine game of whist with several residents, and I knew in any event the way.

Murphy gazed about as we entered the grounds, and I realized he had never been here. I tried not to rush him through—Battersea was a sip to be savored—but I was in a terrible hurry all the same.

When I reached Kiki B's bungalow, Murphy had fallen some way behind. I waved at him, to show him the way, and then knocked on the door.

There was no answer.

Why had I brought no snacks.

I knocked again to no avail. I made some succulent chewing sounds approximating, I thought, quite miraculously the particular timbre of deviled eggs, but they were either not very well-executed and so fooling no one, or, more likely, not quite loud enough to be heard through the doorway.

Finally, I just turned the doorknob and, finding no resistance, entered the room.

Kiki B was gone. Her robe hung upon its hook, her too-big boots sat facing their wall, still enduring this crude punishment, and her bed was neatly made with only a slight indentation to show she'd been there at all.

I am first and foremost an Investigator, despite recent setbacks. I felt the indented quilt for warmth.

It was indeed warm. The bed had been only recently vacated.

Then I noticed a glint of blue, up near the pillows.

It was Kiki B's bracelet, with a shriveled bit of what was now raisin nestled in its prongs. This once great grape, withered and without a fight, fell from its too-big cage as I picked it up. Underneath where the bracelet had lain was a folded-up piece of paper, with MURPHY scrawled across it. This I picked up as well, and holding these scraps of the missing Kiki B, turned toward the door where Murphy had just appeared, eyes shining with the reflected wonders of the place.

—She's not here, I said. —It's odd she left this.

I held up the bracelet.

Murphy came closer. He jangled excitedly. He examined the bracelet up close, giving special attention to its invisible missing jewel. Then he reached into his pocket and pulled out a handful of marbles. He picked through these like an alert little bird, and at last held up a single green stone.

Like a magician, he held the stone up for my scrutiny. Nothing fishy, he might have said, if he'd spoken. No tricks up my sleeve. And then he popped that stone right into the empty prongs of the brace-let, where it nestled as comfortably as an eye in its socket.

He gave me a triumphant look. Ta-da, he might have said though he still said nothing.

When I continued to simply grip the bracelet between my fin-gers, Murphy sighed just a little. He was terrifically long-suffering. He took it from my fingers and slid it over my hand and onto my wrist.

I shook it around a little. It was most pleasing. In heft and weight, in size and shape, in fit and overall aspect, indeed, it was a most pleasing thing.

A most pleasing *accoutrement*.

But if one uses such a high class of word, a word in need of italic, of explanation, one can hardly expect to be understood.

It was a most pleasing thing, which fit. Perfectly, as though it had been mine all along.

It had, Kiki B would have said. Aren't you glad, she would have added, had she not been quite so very gone.

# 76

**It took us some time** to catch our train.

It took us several days at least, if not a week.

Most likely a week.

Our intent had been to simply pick up our things from Tiki Ty's Tiki Barn and perhaps catch our train before anyone had even returned from the bowling emporium.

It was an excellent intent.

I'm proud still of that intent we showed, that focused determination, that unstoppable resolve.

We should likely not have stopped so soon for a shrimp cocktail.

Binelli found us in Monster Waves, glutted on shrimps, an emptied vat of Tiki Ty's dipping and endless opalescent vertebrae littering the area about us, crunching pinkly underfoot.

It was to be expected, which made it no less unpleasant.

Binelli carried an immense bowling trophy.

Our doubles had returned with Binelli, along with the art interns and their spangled gloves, and they all stood rather awkwardly about the books and memorabilias, seeming to browse and adopting postures of casual indifference. The doubles proved in fact better at these postures than the interns, who admittedly had to work twice as hard, required to not only maintain their own postures but those as well of the doubles. No one was quite adept enough to pull it off with any sincerity. If one were in the habit of feeling pity toward inanimate objects—which admittedly I am, though usually and in all honesty only those without faces—one might have felt sorry enough for the doubles to have invited them into the kitchen for a shrimp.

However.

I am one but not that one, just then, and the conversation was terse and confrontational enough to demand my full attention. In that Binelli was preferring that Murphy and I not so much catch a train but rather that we remain at Tiki Ty's until such a time as the next place was determined, and then accompany Binelli to that next place, accept our respective Assignments as per usual, and not be so *disjunctive* all the time.

Binelli's emphasis.

—And what kind of Investigators don't notice bowling balls in the pillows, he went on, fishing about his pockets.

The pillows had yes been heavy, in the hauling stages.

It would yes have been prudent to Investigate.

Binelli found what he was looking for, which was a large tin of polishing and the polishing cloths I had procured for him some time ago, with much difficulty and at grievous personal expense. He stroked his trophy adoringly with the polishing.

What kind of Investigators indeed.

He buffed it with care.

An equally confrontational conversation was occurring quite loudly over in Mediterranean Noir between Odille and Rogan. That conversation went much the same way, in that Rogan was preferring that Odille stay in her usual circumstances and Odille was preferring very much to alter them, according to the new information.

Odille, with the new information, was preferring Binelli.

—I can't believe, she said to Rogan, —that you Puppeted my parents.

—I had to practice, Rogan said. —I knew them so well already.

—I thought they were getting old, Odille said, disgusted. —Old and feeble.

—They were, Rogan agreed, —early models. To see if what Binelli needed could even be done. It was also, he added in his defense, —sort of harder to do people I knew so well. I mean, it's easy to copy basic mannerisms, but to really get someone? They were tricky.

I hoped with sudden urgency that the Professor would remember Dame Uppal's birthday with a fête.

—Well my father, Odille said, —will be crushed. Having his Puppets used that way. He really thought you—

—I really did, Rogan said. He moved a hand up to brush a severe stray shock of hair from Odille's cheek. —I really do.

Odille smiled almost sweetly at him then slapped his hand away. —Well I don't. Find yourself a new muse.

I tilted my head coyly toward Rogan.

He stared quickly and with complete absorption away from me and into the empty vat of dipping for the remainder of his conversation with Odille, which seemed not to bother Odille, as she had finished.

Murphy and I made to gather our things once Binelli's invective reached the stage where he was no longer so much aware of our remaining on its receiving end. We gathered the fine blue pillow, for one, and some shrimps for the trip.

I started to gather as well my fine lotions and cleansers et cetera but Murphy stopped me at the shampooing.

—I think, he said, —it's making your hair red.

I considered this.

Some things became clear.

Then, as I considered further, some more.

—I think, I said, —they might also be erasing my freckles.

I showed him the tiny swatch of spots along the edge of my forehead and he smiled. —I wondered if they'd gone for good, he said. —It was terribly disappointing.

Binelli paced behind us as we went about our gathering. He fumed, and then moped, and then when the conversation between

Odille and Rogan had gasped its last tubercular breath and with a final sigh died, Binelli brightened and rushed away from us and toward Odille's retreating back, forgetting evidently his ire.

Then it was The Lamb's turn to fume, then mope. She had not the benefit however of a furiously confrontational conversation to freely fume and mope within, and her fuming then moping had not much choice other than to extinguish itself fairly quickly and with some throat-clearing embarrassment. Had she been a faceless inanimate object I might have felt sorry for her.

However.

—There are plenty more of us to go around anyhow, Murphy said, once we were settled comfortably in our train car.

He was quite right. My double had been looking with interest after The Lamb as she stomped and fretted her way toward the kitchen, in search no doubt of cake. I might as well admit at this point that I snatched some of my double's wonderful wardrobe from her satchel when she with admirable stealth disappeared in the same direction. The clothes after all were tailored to my perfect dimensions, and finer, yes, than mine. Quite fine.

# 77

The train was bound for tropical climes.

Or so the newly wedded couple sharing our dining car claimed. The bride took a real shine to me and was loving nothing more than to show me over and over again her spectacular ring. It filled her with such joy to have me exclaim over it and examine its facets. She held her doll-like hand up to the window so we could watch how the light played off it, sending spangled diamond reflections all through the car.

It became, true, a tedious sort of entertainment, but they were pleasant enough company, and painted a fine picture for us of black sand beaches and flat white houses set precariously into the cliffs.

A boisterous party of retirees was equally certain that the train was bound for a wild and degenerate riverboat casino. They hoped in fact we'd bet them on it. They hoped to get their betting instinct in shape, they said, so as to be in their best form by the time they reached the tables.

Though I was magnificently garbed in a Mexican wedding dress of splendid ivory cotton—perfect I thought for all those bright white villas stacked up against the sea—I thought a floating casino sounded nice as well.

Murphy shook his head.

—Don't I like to gamble, I said.

—You love to gamble, he said. —Trapped afloat with you in a betting vessel would be tragic.

I toyed with a bit of frayed embroidery at my neckline.

—So you know all about me, I said.

Murphy nodded with a knowing aspect.

The embroidery was lime and yellow and fuchsia. It was a fine embroidery. I wondered had Tiki Ty helped with the wardrobes? Or had Rogan brought in an Italian.

An Italian would never have deigned to tailor a Mexican wedding dress, fine though its embroidery might be.

The diamond's blinding refractions halted further reflection on my embroidery. I groped about and found a great pocket ingeniously obscured by pleating. I pulled out some enormous aviator sunglasses, made just for my face.

—So you know what was my name, I said to Murphy, —then, before Finley.

Tiki Ty must have had a hand in those pockets.

Murphy nodded again and made to speak.

I stopped him. —Don't tell me, I said. —I like Finley quite well.

Murphy made a face of mild distaste. He took on a petulant aspect and stared out the window.

I would be quite immovable on the matter of my name and would not no matter how petulant Murphy's aspect alter my thoughts on this, but I hoped all the same he would not stare out the window for very long.

—Did you say you'd been in a blimp, I said, trying to nudge the conversation in a less controversial direction, but Murphy's petulance knew no bounds.

We'd been beyond the gravel for some time, and had passed through some familiar-seeming swamplands and then sand. We were over water now, with the assistance of an elevated track, and I could see what looked like grass ahead.

When it became quite long that Murphy was staring petulantly out the window, I suggested we enjoy aloud the note we'd found at Battersea. I passed the tantalizing page several times across the very edges of his peripheral vision, and though it was not, being paper, so very shiny, and didn't jangle at all, Murphy couldn't help but grab for it.

# 78

**The Contents of Kiki B's Third Note:**

> A damsel was once in distress
> But lo! she was so red of tress
> That the thought she could be
> The part missing from me
> Makes me shudder a bit, I confess.

# 79

—So she was, I said.

I began again.

—So I am, I said, —quite mad then. Now that we are only me.

—I think she was not, Murphy said, —quite mad.

He looked again over the note.

—It makes pretty good sense, he said. —If you think for instance of photographic negatives.

—It was anyway meant for me, he said.

—Not that I hadn't been already quite aware, he said. —But it was valiant of her to try, lest I hadn't been.

He hummed his smug little three-note tune.

—What is that you're always humming, I said.

—You don't remember anything, he said. —*Finley,* he added with great distaste.

He sang the words: —O-*ri*-on you-*came*-and you-*took*-all my-*mar*-bles.

—Ring any bells, he said after.

I shook my head.

Then I remembered something.

Not something from before, like he wanted me to, but something all the same.

I shuffled through Lavendar's satchel and produced the slip of paper Odille had so painstakingly bisected at the restaurant, miraculously unmolested.

—It was meant to be a code, I said, —but we never got to use it. It's the same thing, right.

Murphy examined it. He filled in the missing words. I was quite correct.

—How did she know your song, I said.

My ire was indisputably up.

—That stupid muse, I said. —Musing all about, indiscriminately.

—Most people know that song, Murphy said. —It's a rather common song. Something you learn in the early levels, Murphy said. —It also goes with an outdoors game.

—It's funny, Murphy said, thinking a bit further on it, —that it was there all along in your pocket.

—Half of it, I said, —anyway.

It would have been, I considered, prudent to have collected Odille's half of the pass-phrase before blowing out of the Tiki Barn. One would think, I considered further, that over the course of an entire week's time, an entire week of Odille ever present in the Tiki Barn and traipsing resplendent about in any number of stunning shoes, one might have found the opportunity to relieve Odille of any stray pieces of Murphy.

All that time spent before the basin glass, watching the freckles grow!

But this thought made me more pleased than irked, and reminded me of something.

—Is my hair really then quite dirty, I said. —Dirty and blond rather than lustrous and red.

—It's the color dirtyblond, Murphy said, —but not always dirty.

He considered for a moment. —Though often *quite* dirty, he said. —Truth be told.

I ignored this blatant misrepresentation.

—And there are many freckles, I said.

—Many, he said. —So many as to be shocking.

I became quite excited. I fussed over Lavendar and Golden. For Golden had been, I perhaps failed to report in all the excitement, nestled in Lavendar's satchel when I snatched it up from the bowling emporium. I'd attributed at the time its heaviness you'll recall to Lavendar's depression and to my own post-Quadrille exhaustion, but it in fact turned out that the beasts had made one another's acquaintance whilst neglected on the snack-bar table and so loathsomely bored.

—I suppose Odille will be made an Investigator, I said, watching Murphy slyly for any hint of reaction. I found none but had already begun the tiresome topic and figured I should see it through. —So there should still be plenty then. For the Assignments.

—There are the Puppets as well, Murphy said. —I'm sure they can be put to work. Those interns don't have anything much better to do.

—They'll probably, I said, —not even be the Most Hated.

That made me think of something else.

—So you know, I said, —why I hate so much the Russians.

Murphy hummed a bit and jangled his pockets.

I waited. I sang the words silently to myself in tune with his humming. The words rang no bells but were a pleasant enough bit of verse.

He knew I would win if he attempted a standoff.

I sang the words a bit out loud, softly.

He stopped humming and sighed and nodded dolefully.

—Do you really want to know, he said.

—Why wouldn't I, I said.

—I want to know everything, I said.

—Except my name, I said. —But everything else.

—I'll tell you, he said, —but you won't like it.

# 80

**He did,** and I didn't.

# 81

**I didn't like it at all.**
 I became quite silent.
 I became quite silent for quite some time.

# 82

**I knew even as it lasted** that it was not a silence like the last great silence. I could feel the train bumping along beneath my seat and hear Murphy putting off the anxious bride who was wondering if I might look at her ring a bit before dinner, and I could sense Lavendar poking his head up from his satchel, making sure I was there as I had gone so still.

I was still there.

And it didn't last so very long, though I perhaps did let it go on a touch longer than its natural life, as a silence can be quite comfortable what with the soft focus and dreamy warmth.

I enjoyed some thinking about very hot sand, and about a riot of freckles, so many as to be shocking. I wondered for a spell whether Tiki Ty would employ his double to help him run the Tiki Barn, send him to Siam for ingredients and such.

I maybe had a very brief nap.

I emerged with only a mild ache around my edges but with no more or less memory than I'd had going in.

Murphy was staring at me anxiously as was Lavendar. Golden did not seem to care one way or the other, but that's to be expected of a snake not your own.

—You're still here then, Murphy said.

He studied my eyes, which would, I have since come to learn, remain yellow.

(Murphy had done his best to console me. —They're how I was sure it was really you.)

One must take the bad with the good.

(—They're not as terrible, Murphy had added, —when the hair's not so red.)

Yellow eyes aren't the worst thing.

Perhaps in Greece yellow eyes will be quite the thing.

—You're here, Murphy said again. —It's okay then.

I supposed it was. And out the window, green began.

First and foremost, to Ben Barnhart who with some silkysmooth combination of incisiveness and wicked wit made me feel throughout this process that not only was I in good hands but had in fact won the editor lottery. And huge thanks to Jessica Deutsch, Daniel Slager, and the entire Milkweed staff toward whom my affections know no bounds.

To Julia Holmes, E. Tyler Lindvall, Christopher Swetala, Hillery Hugg, Claire Gutierrez, and Mark Binelli whose writing, reading, and friendship are unrivaled; to the truly fabulous Lauren Bailey, Marina Shiah, Tina Wang, and all the burgers—my happiest accident; and to Luke Zaleski and the exceptionally dapper staff of *GQ* who I'm terrifically lucky to know.

To the Murphys, who've been a second family; and to my own whole family, too many to name but in particular Deb and Dean Fanucci, Chris Lavelle, and Kim Sperandeo, godmothers (and, ah, godfather) of the highest caliber.

And to Laura, Fergus, and Caitlin Henehan. There aren't words enough for the support, compassion, wit, and beauty of this dazzling gang of family. For maintaining faith in me and my work—in the face of any and all available evidence to the contrary—I can't thank you enough; for making the whole ride a riot, I'm truly, everlastingly grateful.

**Kira Henehan** was born in New York and grew up in various locales around the U.S., Canada, and the Caribbean. Her work has been published in *Fence, jubilat, Chelsea, Conjunctions,* and *Denver Quarterly,* among others, and has received a Pushcart Prize and been included in *A Best of Fence: The First Nine Years* anthology. She attended San Francisco State University and Columbia University, and lives in New York City. This is her first novel.

## More Fiction from Milkweed Editions

To order books or for more information,
contact Milkweed at (800) 520-6455
or visit our Web site (www.milkweed.org).

*Visigoth*
Gary Amdahl

*The Farther Shore*
Matthew Eck

*Thirst*
Ken Kalfun

*Aquaboogie*
Susan Straight

## Milkweed Editions

Founded in 1979, Milkweed Editions is one of the largest independent, nonprofit literary publishers in the United States. Milkweed publishes with the intention of making a humane impact on society, in the belief that good writing can transform the human heart and spirit.

## Join Us

Milkweed depends on the generosity of foundations and individuals like you, in addition to the sales of its books. In an increasingly consolidated and bottom-line-driven publishing world, your support allows us to select and publish books on the basis of their literary quality and the depth of their message. Please visit our Web site (www.milkweed.org) or contact us at (800) 520-6455 to learn more about our donor program.

Milkweed Editions, a nonprofit publisher, gratefully acknowledges sustaining support from Emilie and Henry Buchwald; the Patrick and Aimee Butler Foundation; the Dougherty Family Foundation; the Ecolab Foundation; the General Mills Foundation; John and Joanne Gordon; William and Jeanne Grandy; the Jerome Foundation; Robert and Stephanie Karon; the Lerner Foundation; Sally Macut; Sanders and Tasha Marvin; the McKnight Foundation; Mid-Continent Engineering; the Minnesota State Arts Board, through an appropriation by the Minnesota State Legislature, a grant from the Wells Fargo Foundation Minnesota, and a grant from the National Endowment for the Arts; Kelly Morrison and John Willoughby; the National Endowment for the Arts, and the American Reinvestment and Recovery Act; the Navarre Corporation; Ann and Doug Ness; Jörg and Angie Pierach; the RBC Foundation USA; Ellen Sturgis; the Target Foundation; the James R. Thorpe Foundation; the Travelers Foundation; Moira and John Turner; and Edward and Jenny Wahl.

THE MᶜKNIGHT FOUNDATION

Interior design by Rachel Holscher
Typeset in Sabon
by BookMobile Design and Publishing Services, Minneapolis
Printed on acid-free 100% post consumer waste paper
by Friesens Corporation

## ENVIRONMENTAL BENEFITS STATEMENT

**Milkweed Editions** saved the following resources by printing the pages of this book on chlorine free paper made with 100% post-consumer waste.

| TREES | WATER | SOLID WASTE | GREENHOUSE GASES |
|-------|-------|-------------|------------------|
| 52 | 23,765 | 1,443 | 4,934 |
| FULLY GROWN | GALLONS | POUNDS | POUNDS |

Calculations based on research by Environmental Defense and the Paper Task Force. Manufactured at Friesens Corporation